Michael Penguyne:
Or, Fisher Life on the Cornish Coast

William Henry Giles Kingston

Copyright © 2019 by ReadAthenaeum.com
All rights reserved. This book or any portion thereof may not be reproduced or used in any manner whatsoever without the express written permission of the publisher except for the use of brief quotations in a book review.

First Printing, 2019

www.readathenaeum.com

Contents

Chapter One 7
Chapter Two 16
Chapter Three 25
Chapter Four 35
Chapter Five 42
Chapter Six 49
Chapter Seven 61
Chapter Eight 74
Chapter Nine 84
Chapter Ten 96

Chapter One.

As the sun rose over the Lizard, the southernmost point of old England, his rays fell on the tanned sails of a fleet of boats bounding lightly across the heaving waves before a fresh westerly breeze. The distant shore, presenting a line of tall cliffs, towards which the boats were steering, still lay in the deepest shade.

Each boat was laden with a large heap of nets and several baskets filled with brightly-shining fish.

In the stern of one, tiller in hand, sat a strongly-built man, whose deeply-furrowed countenance and grizzled hair showed that he had been for many a year a toiler on the ocean. By his side was a boy of about twelve years of age, dressed in flushing coat and sou'wester, busily employed with a marline-spike, in splicing an eye to a rope's-end.

The elder fisherman, now looking up at his sails, now stooping down to get a glance beneath them at the shore, and then turning his head towards the south-west, where heavy clouds were gathering fast, meanwhile cast an approving look at the boy.

"Ye are turning in that eye smartly and well, Michael," he said. "Whatever you do, try and do it in that fashion. It has been my wish to teach you what is right as well as I know it. Try not only to please man, my boy, but to love and serve God, whose eye is always on you. Don't forget the golden rule either: 'Do to others as you would they should do to you.'"

"I have always wished to understand what you have told me, and tried to obey you, father," said the boy.

"You have been a good lad, Michael, and have more than repaid me for any trouble you may have caused me. You are getting a big boy now, though, and it's time that you should know certain matters about yourself which no one else is so well able to tell you as I am."

The boy looked up from his work, wondering what Paul Trefusis was going to say.

"You know, lad, that you are called Michael Penguyne, and that my name is Paul Trefusis. Has it never crossed your mind that though I have always treated you as a son—and you have ever behaved towards me as a good and dutiful son should behave—that you were not really my own child?"

"To say the truth, I have never thought about it, father," answered the boy, looking up frankly in the old man's face. "I am oftener called Trefusis than Penguyne, so I fancied that Penguyne was another name tacked on to Michael, and that Trefusis was just as much my name as yours. And oh! father, I would rather be your child than the son of anybody else."

"There is no harm in wishing that, Michael; but it's as well that you should know the real state of the case, and as I cannot say what may happen to me, I do not wish to put off telling you any longer. I am not as strong and young as I once was, and maybe God will think fit to take me away before I have reached the threescore years and ten which He allows some to live. We should not put off doing to another time what can be done now, and so you see I wish to say what has been on my mind to tell you for many a day past, though I have not liked to say it, lest it should in any way grieve you. You promise me, Michael, you won't let it do that? You know how much I and granny and Nelly love you, and will go on loving you as much as ever."

"I know you do, father, and so do granny and Nelly; I am sure they love me," said the boy gazing earnestly into Paul's face, with wonder and a shade of sorrow depicted on his own countenance.

"That's true," said Paul. "But about what I was going to say to you.

"My wife, who is gone to heaven, Nelly's mother, and I,

never had another child but her. Your father, Michael, as truehearted a seaman as ever stepped, had been my friend and shipmate for many a long year. We were bred together, and had belonged to the same boat fishing off this coast till we were grown men, when at last we took it into our heads to wish to visit foreign climes, and so we went to sea together. After knocking about for some years, and going to all parts of the world, we returned home, and both fell in love, and married. Your mother was an orphan, without kith or kin, that your father could hear of—a good, pretty girl she was, and worthy of him.

"We made up our minds that we would stay on shore and follow our old calling and look after our wives and families. We had saved some money, but it did not go as far as we thought it would, and we agreed that if we could make just one more trip to sea, we should gain enough for what we wanted.

"You were about two years old, and my Nelly was just born.

"We went to Falmouth, where ships often put in, wanting hands, and masters are ready to pay good wages to obtain them. We hadn't been there a day, when we engaged on board a ship bound out to the West Indies. As she was not likely to be long absent, this just suited us. Your father got a berth as third mate, for he was the best scholar, and I shipped as boatswain.

"We made the voyage out, and had just reached the chops of the Channel, coming back, bound for Bristol, and hoping in a few days to be home again with our wives, when thick weather came on, and a heavy gale of wind sprang up. It blew harder and harder. Whether or not the captain was out of his reckoning I cannot say, but I suspect he was. Before long, our sails were blown away, and our foremast went by the board. We did our best to keep the ship off the shore, for all know well that it is about as dangerous a one as is to be found round England.

"The night was dark as pitch, the gale still increasing.

"'Paul,' said your father to me as we were standing together, 'you and I may never see another sun rise; but still one of us may escape. You remember the promise we made each other.'

"'Yes, Michael,' I said, 'that I do, and hope to keep it.'

"The promise was that if one should be lost and the other saved, he who escaped should look after the wife and family of the one who was lost.

"I had scarcely answered him when the look-out forward shouted 'Breakers ahead!' and before the ship's course could be altered, down she came, crashing on the rocks. It was all up with the craft; the seas came dashing over her, and many of those on deck were washed away. The unfortunate passengers rushed up from below, and in an instant were swept overboard.

"The captain ordered the remaining masts to be cut away, to ease the ship; but it did no good, and just as the last fell she broke in two, and all on board were cast into the water, I found myself clinging with your father to one of the masts. The head of the mast was resting on a rock. We made our way along it; I believed that others were following; but just as we reached the rock the mast was carried away, and he and I found that we alone had escaped.

"The seas rose up foaming around us, and every moment we expected to be washed away. Though we knew many were perishing close around us we had no means of helping them. All we could do was to cling on and try and save our own lives.

"'I hope we shall get back home yet, Michael,' I said, wishing to cheer your father, for he was more down-hearted than usual.

"'I hope so, Paul, but I don't know; God's will be done, whatever that will is. Paul, you will meet me in heaven, I hope,' he answered, for he was a Christian man. 'If I am taken, you will look after Mary and my boy,' he added. Again I promised him, and I knew to a certainty that he would look after my Nelly, should he be saved and I drowned.

"When the morning came at last scarcely a timber or plank of the wreck was to be seen. What hope of escape had either of us? The foaming waters raged around, and we were half perished with cold and hunger. On looking about I found a small spar washed up on the rock, and, fastening our handkerchiefs together, we rigged out a flag, but there was little chance of a boat putting off in such weather and coming near enough to see it. We now knew that we were not far off the Land's End, on one of two rocks called The Sisters, with the village of Senum abreast of us.

"Your father and I looked in each other's faces; we felt that there was little hope that we should ever see our wives and infants again. Still we spoke of the promise we had made each other—not that there was any need of that, for we neither of us were likely to forget it.

"The spring tides were coming on, and though we had escaped as yet, the sea might before long break over the rock and carry us away. Even if it did not we must die of hunger and thirst, should no craft come to our rescue.

"We kept our eyes fixed on the distant shore; they ached with the strain we put on them, as we tried to make out whether any boat was being launched to come off to us.

"A whole day passed—another night came on. We did not expect to see the sun rise again. Already the seas as they struck the rock sent the foam flying over us, and again and again washed up close to where we were sitting.

"Notwithstanding our fears, daylight once more broke upon us, but what with cold and hunger we were well-nigh dead.

"Your father was a stronger man than I fancied myself, and yet he now seemed most broken down. He could scarcely stand to wave our flag.

"The day wore on, the wind veered a few points to the nor'ard, and the sun burst out now and then from among the clouds, and, just as we were giving up all hope, his light fell on the sails of a boat which had just before put off from the shore. She breasted the waves bravely. Was she, though, coming towards us? We could not have been seen so far off. Still on she came, the wind allowing her to be close-hauled to steer towards the rock. The tide meantime was rapidly rising. If she did not reach us soon, we knew too well that the sea would come foaming over the rock and carry us away.

"I stood up and waved our flag. Still the boat stood on; the spray was beating in heavy showers over her, and it was as much as she could do to look up to her canvas. Sometimes as I watched her I feared that the brave fellows who were coming to our rescue would share the fate which was likely to befall us. She neared the rock. I tried to cheer up your father.

"'In five minutes we shall be safe on board, Michael,' I said.

"'Much may happen in five minutes, Paul; but you will not forget my Mary and little boy,' he answered.

"'No fear of that,' I said; 'but you will be at home to look after them yourself.'

"I tried to cheer as the boat came close to the rock, but my voice failed me.

"The sails were lowered and she pulled in. A rope was hove, and I caught it. I was about to make it fast round your father.

"'You go first, Paul,' he said. 'If you reach the boat I will try to follow, but there is no use for me to try now; I should be drowned before I got half way.'

"Still I tried to secure the rope round him, but he resisted all my efforts. At last I saw that I must go, or we should both be lost, and I hoped to get the boat in nearer and to return with a second rope to help him.

"I made the rope fast round my waist and plunged in. I had hard work to reach the boat; I did not know how weak I was. At last I was hauled on board, and was singing out for a rope, when the people in the boat uttered a cry, and looking up I saw a huge sea come rolling along. Over the rock it swept, taking off your poor father. I leapt overboard with the rope still round my waist, in the hopes of catching him, but in a moment he was hidden from my sight, and, more dead than alive, I was again hauled on board.

"The crew of the boat pulled away from the rock; they knew that all hopes of saving my friend were gone. Sail was made, and we stood for the shore.

"The people at the village attended me kindly, but many days passed before I was able to move.

"As soon as I had got strength enough, with a sad heart I set out homewards. How could I face your poor mother, and tell her that her husband was gone? I would send my own dear wife, I thought, to break the news to her.

"As I reached my own door I heard a child's cry; it was that of my little Nelly, and granny's voice trying to soothe her.

"I peeped in at the window. There sat granny, with the child on her knee, but my wife was not there. She has gone to market, I thought. Still my heart sank within me. I gained courage to go in.

"'Where is Nelly?' I asked, as granny, with the baby in her arms, rose to meet me.

"'Here is the only Nelly you have got, my poor Paul,' she said, giving me the child.

"I felt as if my heart would break. I could not bring myself to ask how or when my wife had died. Granny told me, however, for she knew it must be told, and the sooner it was over the better. She had been taken with a fever soon after I had left home.

"It was long before I recovered myself.

"'I must go and tell the sad news I bring to poor Mary,' I said.

"Granny shook her head.

"'She is very bad, it will go well-nigh to kill her outright,' she observed.

"I would have got granny to go, but I wanted to tell your poor mother of my promise to your father, and, though it made my heartache, I determined to go myself.

"I found her, with you by her side.

"'Here is father,' you cried out, but your mother looked up, and seemed to know in a moment what had happened.

"'Where is Michael?' she asked.

"'You know, Mary, your husband and I promised to look after each other's children, if one was taken and the other left; and I mean to keep my promise to look after you and your little boy.'

"Your mother knew, by what I said, that your father was gone.

"'God's will be done,' she murmured; 'He knows what is best—I hope soon to be with him.'

"Before the month was out we carried your poor mother to her grave, and I took you to live with granny and Nelly.

"There, Michael, you know all I can tell you about yourself. I have had hard times now and then, but I have done my duty to you; and I say again, Michael, you have always been a good and dutiful boy, and not a fault have I had to find with you."

"Thank you, father, for saying that; and you will still let me call you father, for I cannot bring myself to believe that I am not really your son."

"That I will, Michael; a son you have always been to me, and my son I wish you to remain. And, Michael, as I have watched over you, so I want you to watch over my little Nelly. Should I be called away, be a brother and true friend to her, for I know not to what dangers she may be exposed. Granny is old, and her years on earth may be few, and when she is gone, Michael, Nelly will have no one to look to but you. She has no kith nor kin, that I know of, able or willing to take care of her. Her mother's brother and only sister went to Australia years ago, and no news has ever come of them since, and my brothers found their graves in the deep sea, so that Nelly will be alone in the world. That is the only thing that troubles me, and often makes me feel sad when we are away at night, and the wind blows strong and the sea runs high, and I think of the many I have known who have lost their lives in stouter boats than mine. But God is merciful; He has promised to take care of the widow and orphan, and He will keep His word. I know that, and so I again look up and try to drive all mistrustful thoughts of His goodness from my mind."

"Father, while I have life I will take care of Nelly, and pray for her, and, if needs be, fight for her," exclaimed Michael.

He spoke earnestly and with all sincerity, for he intended, God willing, to keep his word.

Chapter Two.

The fleet of fishing-boats as they approached the coast steered in different directions, some keeping towards Kynance and Landewednach, while Paul Trefusis shaped his course for Mullyan Cove, towards the north, passing close round the lofty Gull Rock, which stands in solitary grandeur far away from the shore, braving the fierce waves as they roll in from the broad Atlantic.

Asparagus Island and Lion Rock opened out to view, while the red and green sides of the precipitous serpentine cliffs could now be distinguished, assuming various fantastic shapes: one shaped into a complete arch, another the form of a gigantic steeple, with several caves penetrating deep into the cliff, on a level with the narrow belt of yellow sand.

Young Michael, though accustomed from his childhood to the wild and romantic scenery, had never passed that way without looking at it with an eye of interest, and wondering how those cliffs and rocks came to assume the curious forms they wore.

The little "Wild Duck," for that was the name Paul Trefusis had given his boat, continued her course, flying before the fast increasing gale close inshore, to avoid the strong tide which swept away to the southward, till, rounding a point, she entered the mouth of a narrow inlet which afforded shelter to a few boats and small craft. It was a wild, almost savage-looking place, though extremely picturesque. On either side were rugged and broken cliffs, in some parts rising sheer out of the water to the gorse-covered downs above, in others broken in terraces and ledges, affording space for a few fishermen's cottages and huts, which were seen perched here and there, looking down on the tranquil water of the harbour.

The inlet made a sharp bend a short distance from its mouth, so that, as Paul's boat proceeded upwards, the view of the sea being completely shut out, it bore the appearance of a lake. At the further end a stream of water came rushing down over the summit of the cliffs, dashing from ledge to ledge, now breaking into masses of foam, now descending perpendicularly many feet, now running along a rapid incline, and serving to turn a small flour-mill built a short way up on the side of the cliff above the harbour.

Steep as were the cliffs, a zigzag road had been cut in them, leading from the downs above almost to the mouth of the harbour, where a rock which rose directly out of the water formed a natural quay, on which the fishing-boats could land their cargoes. Beyond this the road was rough and steep, and fitted only for people on foot, or donkeys with their panniers, to go up and down. Art had done little to the place.

The little "Wild Duck," a few moments before tossed and tumbled by the angry seas, now glided smoothly along for a few hundred yards, when the sails were lowered, and she floated up to a dock between two rocks. Hence, a rough pathway led from one of the cottages perched on the side of the cliff. At a distance it could scarcely have been distinguished from the cliff itself. Its walls were composed of large blocks of unhewn serpentine, masses of clay filling up the interstices, while it was roofed with a thick dark thatch, tightly fastened down with ropes, and still further secured by slabs of stone to prevent its being carried away by the fierce blasts which are wont to sweep up and down the ravine in winter.

There was space enough on either side of the cottage for a small garden, which appeared to be carefully cultivated, and was enclosed by a stone wall. At the upper part of the pathway a flight of steps, roughly hewn in the rock, led to the cottage door.

The door opened as soon as Paul's boat rounded the point, and a young girl with a small creel or fish basket at her back was seen lightly tripping down the pathway, followed by an old woman, who, though she supported her steps with a staff, also carried a creel of the ordinary size. She wore a large broad-brimmed black hat, and a gaily-coloured calico jacket over her winsey skirt; an apron, and shoes with metal buckles, completing the ordinary costume of a fish-wife of that district. Little Nelly was dressed very like her grandmother, except that her feet were bare, and that she had a necklace of small shells round her throat. Her face was pretty and intelligent, her well-browned cheeks glowed with the hue of health, her eyes were large and grey, and her black hair, drawn up off her forehead, hung in neat plaits tied with ribbons behind her back. Nelly Trefusis was indeed a good specimen of a young fisher-girl.

She tripped lightly down the pathway, springing to the top of the outermost rock just before her father's boat glided by it, and in an instant stepping nimbly on board, she threw herself into his arms and bestowed a kiss on his weather-beaten brow.

Michael had leaped on shore to fend off the boat, so that he lost the greeting she would have given him.

"You have had a good haul with the nets to-night, father," she said, looking into the baskets; "Granny and I can scarce carry half of them to market, and unless Abel Mawgan the hawker comes in time to buy them, you and Michael will have work to do to salt them down."

"It is well that we should have had a good haul, Nelly, for dirty weather is coming on, and it may be many a day before we are able to cast our nets again," answered Paul, looking up affectionately at his child, while he began with a well-practised hand to stow the boat's sail.

Nelly meantime was filling her creel with fish, that she might lessen the weight of the baskets which her father and Michael had to lift on shore. As soon as it was full she stepped back on the rock, giving a kiss to Michael as she passed him.

The baskets were soon landed, and the creel being filled,

she and Nelly ascended the hill, followed by Paul and Michael, who, carrying the baskets between them, brought up the remainder of the fish.

Breakfast, welcome to those who had been toiling all night, had been placed ready on the table, and leaving Paul and his boy to discuss it, Polly Lanreath, as the old dame was generally called, and her little granddaughter, set off on their long journey over the downs to dispose of their fish at Helston, or at the villages and the few gentlemen's houses they passed on their way. It was a long distance for the old woman and girl to go, but they went willingly whenever fish had been caught, for they depended on its sale for their livelihood, and neither Paul nor Michael could have undertaken the duty, nor would they have sold the fish so well as the dame and Nelly, who were welcomed whenever they appeared. Their customers knew that they could depend on their word when they mentioned the very hour when the fish were landed.

The old dame's tongue wagged cheerfully as she walked along with Nelly by her side, and she often beguiled the way with tales and anecdotes of bygone days, and ancient Cornish legends which few but herself remembered. Nelly listened with eager ears, and stored away in her memory all she heard, and often when they got back in the evening she would beg her granny to recount again for the benefit of her father and Michael the stories she had told in the morning.

She had a cheerful greeting, too, for all she met; for some she had a quiet joke; for the giddy and careless a word of warning, which came with good effect from one whom all respected. At the cottages of the poor she was always a welcome visitor, while at the houses of the more wealthy she was treated with courtesy and kindness; and many a housewife who might have been doubtful about buying fish that day, when the dame and her granddaughter arrived, made up her mind to assist in lightening Nelly's creel by selecting some of its contents.

The dame, as her own load decreased, would always insist on taking some of her granddaughter's, deeming that the little maiden had enough to do to trot on so many miles by her side, without having to carry a burden on her back in addition. Nelly would declare that she did not feel the weight, but the sturdy old dame generally gained her point, though she might consent to replenish Nelly's basket before entering the town, for some of their customers preferred the fish which the bright little damsel offered them for sale to those in her grandmother's creel.

Thus, though their daily toil was severe, and carried on under summer's sun, or autumn's gales, and winter's rain and sleet, they themselves were ever cheerful and contented, and seldom failed to return home with empty creels and well-filled purses.

Paul Trefusis might thus have been able to lay by a store for the time when the dame could no longer trudge over the country as she had hitherto done, and he unable to put off with nets or lines to catch fish; but often for weeks together the gales of that stormy coast prevented him from venturing to sea, and the vegetables and potatoes produced in his garden, and the few fish he and Michael could catch in the harbour, were insufficient to support their little household, so that at the end of each year Paul found himself no richer than at the beginning.

While Nelly and her grandmother and the other women of the village were employed in selling the fish, the men had plenty of occupation during the day in drying and mending their nets, and repairing their boats, while some time was required to obtain the necessary sleep of which their nightly toil had deprived them. Those toilers of the sea were seldom idle. When bad weather prevented them from going far from the coast, they fished with lines, or laid down their lobster-pots among the rocks close inshore, while occasionally a few fish were to be caught in the waters of their little harbour. Most of them also cultivated patches of ground on the sides of the valley which opened out at the further end of the gorge, but, except potatoes, their fields afforded but precarious crops.

Paul and Michael had performed most of their destined task: the net had been spread along the rocks to dry, and two or three rents, caused by the fisherman's foes, some huge conger or cod-fish, had been repaired. A portion of their fish had been sold to Abel Mawgan, and the remainder had been salted for their own use, when Paul, who had been going about his work with less than his usual spirit, complained of pains in his back and limbs. Leaving Michael to clean out the boat and moor her, and to bring up the oars and other gear, he went into the cottage to lie down and rest.

Little perhaps did the strong and hardy fisherman suppose, as he threw himself on his bunk in the little chamber where he and Michael slept, that he should never again rise, and that his last trip on the salt sea had been taken—that for the last time he had hauled his nets, that his life's work was done. Yet he might have had some presentiment of what was going to happen as he sailed homewards that morning, when he resolved to tell Michael about his parents, and gave him the account of his father's death which has been described.

The young fisher boy went on board the "Wild Duck," and was busily employed in cleaning her out, thinking over what he had heard in the morning. Whilst thus engaged, he saw a small boat coming down from the head of the harbour towards him, pulled by a lad somewhat older than himself.

"There is Eban Cowan, the miller's son. I suppose he is coming here. I wonder what he wants?" he thought. "The 'Polly' was out last night, and got a good haul, so it cannot be for fish."

Michael was right in supposing that Eban Cowan was coming to their landing-place. The lad in the punt pulled up alongside the "Wild Duck."

"How fares it with you, Michael?" he said, putting out his hand. "You did well this morning, I suspect, like most of us. Did Abel Mawgan buy all your 'catch'? He took the whole of ours."

"No, granny and Nelly started off to Helston with their creels full, as they can get a much better price than Mawgan will give," answered Michael.

"I am sorry that Nelly is away, for I have brought her some shells I promised her a month ago. But as I have nothing to do, I will bide with you till she comes back."

"She and granny won't be back till late, I am afraid, and you lose your time staying here," said Michael.

"Never mind, I will lend you a hand," said Eban, making his punt fast, and stepping on board the "Wild Duck."

He was a fine, handsome, broad-shouldered lad, with dark eyes and hair, and with a complexion more like that of an inhabitant of the south than of an English boy.

He took up a mop as he spoke, whisking up the bits of seaweed and fish-scales which covered the bottom of the boat.

"Thank you," said Michael; "I won't ask you to stop, for I must go and turn in and get some sleep. Father does not seem very well, and I shall have more work in the evening."

"What is the matter with Uncle Paul?" asked Eban.

Michael told him that he had been complaining since the morning, but he hoped the night's rest would set him to rights.

"You won't want to go to sea to-night. It's blowing hard outside, and likely to come on worse," observed Eban.

Though he called Paul "uncle," there was no relationship. He merely used the term of respect common in Cornwall when a younger speaks of an older man.

Eban, however, did not take Michael's hint, but continued working away in the boat till she was completely put to rights.

"Now," he said, "I will help you up with the oars and

sails. You have more than enough to do, it seems to me, for a small fellow like you."

"I am able to do it," answered Michael; "and I am thankful that I can."

"You live hard, though, and your father grows no richer," observed Eban. "If he did as others do, and as my father has advised him many a time, he would be a richer man, and you and your sister and Aunt Lanreath would not have to toil early and late, and wear the life out of you as you do. I hope you will be wiser."

"I know my father is right, whatever he does, and I hope to follow his example," answered Michael, unstepping the mast, which he let fall on his shoulder preparatory to carrying it up to the shed.

"I was going to take that up," said Eban; "it is too heavy for you by half."

"It is my duty, thank you," said Michael, somewhat coldly, stepping on shore with his burden.

Slight as he looked, he carried the heavy spar up the pathway and deposited it against the side of the house. He was returning for the remainder of the boat's gear, when he met Eban with it on his shoulders.

"Thank you," he said; "but I don't want to give you my work to do."

"It's no labour to me," answered Eban. "Just do you go and turn in, and I will moor the boat and make a new set of 'tholes' for you."

Again Michael begged that his friend would not trouble himself, adding—

"If you have brought the shells for Nelly and will leave them with me, I will give them to her when she comes home."

Nothing he could say, however, would induce Eban to go away. The latter had made up his mind to remain till Nelly's return.

Still Michael was not to be turned from his purpose of doing his own work, though he could not prevent Eban from assisting him; and not till the boat was moored, and her gear deposited in the shed, would he consent to enter the cottage and seek the rest he required.

Meantime Eban, returning to his punt, shaped out a set of new tholes as he proposed, and then set off up the hill, hoping to meet Nelly and her grandmother.

He must have found them, for after some time he again came down the hill in their company, talking gaily, now to one, now to the other. He was evidently a favourite with the old woman.

Nelly thanked him with a sweet smile for the shells, which he had collected in some of the sandy little bays along the coast, which neither she nor Michael had ever been able to visit.

She was about to invite him into, the cottage, when Michael appeared at the door, saying, with a sad face—

"O granny! I am so thankful you are come; father seems very bad, and groans terribly. I never before saw him in such a way, and have not known what to do."

Nelly on this darted in, and was soon by Paul's bedside, followed by her grandmother.

Eban lingered about outside waiting. Michael at length came out to him again.

"There is no use waiting," he said; and Eban, reluctantly going down to his boat, pulled away up the harbour.

Chapter Three.

Paul continued to suffer much during the evening; still he would not have the doctor sent for. "I shall get better maybe soon, if it's God's will, though such pains are new to me," he said, groaning as he spoke.

The storm which had been threatening now burst with unusual strength. Michael, with the assistance of Nelly and her grandmother, got in the nets in time.

All hope of doing anything on the water for that night, at all events, must be abandoned; the weather was even too bad to allow Michael to fish in the harbour.

Little Nelly's young heart was deeply grieved as she heard her father groan with pain—he who had never had a day's illness that she could recollect. Nothing the dame could think of relieved him.

The howling of the wind, the roaring of the waves as they dashed against the rock-bound coast, the pattering of the rain, and ever and anon the loud claps of thunder which echoed among the cliffs, made Nelly's heart sink within her. Often it seemed as if the very roof of the cottage would be blown off. Still she was thankful that her father and Michael were inside instead of buffeting the foaming waves out at sea.

If careful tending could have done Paul good he would soon have got well. The old dame seemed to require no sleep, and she would scarcely let either of her grandchildren take her place even for a few minutes. Though she generally went marketing, rather than leave her charge she sent Michael and Nelly to buy bread and other necessaries at the nearest village, which was, however, at some distance.

The rain had ceased, but the wind blew strong over the wild moor.

"I am afraid father is going to be very ill," observed Michael. "He seemed to think something was going to happen to him when he told me what I did not know before about myself. Have you heard anything about it, Nelly?"

"What is it?" asked Nelly; "till you tell me I cannot say."

"You've always thought that I was your brother, Nelly, haven't you?"

"As to that, I have always loved you as a brother, and whether one or no, that should not make you unhappy. Has father said anything to you about it?"

"Yes. He said that I was not your brother; and he has told me all about my father and mother: how my father was drowned, and my mother died of a broken heart. I could well-nigh have cried when I heard the tale."

Nelly looked up into Michael's face.

"It's no news to me," she said. "Granny told me of it some time ago, but I begged her not to let you find it out lest it should make you unhappy, and you should fancy we were not going to love you as much as we have always done. But, Michael, don't go and fancy that; though you are not my brother, I will love you as much as ever, as long as you live: for, except father and granny, I have no friend but you in the world."

"I will be your brother and your true friend as long as I live, Nelly," responded Michael; "still I would rather have thought myself to be your brother, that I might have a better right to work for you, and fight for you too, if needs be."

"You will do that, I know, Michael," said Nelly, "whatever may happen."

Michael felt that he should be everything that was bad if he did not, though it did not occur to him to make any great promises of what he would do.

They went on talking cheerfully and happily together, for though Nelly was anxious about her father, she did not yet understand how ill he was.

They procured the articles for which they had been sent,

and, laden with them, returned homewards. They were making their way along one of the hedges which divide the fields in that part of Cornwall—not composed of brambles but of solid rock, and so broad that two people can walk abreast without fear of tumbling off—and were yet some distance from the edge of the ravine down which they had to go to their home, when they saw Eban Cowan coming towards them.

"I wish he had gone some other way," said Nelly. "He is very kind bringing me shells and other things, but, Michael, I do not like him. I do not know what it is, but there is something in the tone of his voice; it's not truthful like yours and father's."

"I never thought about that. He is a bold-hearted, good-natured fellow," observed Michael. "He has always been inclined to like us, and shown a wish to be friendly."

"I don't want to make him suppose that we are not friendly," said Nelly; "only still—"

She was unable to finish the sentence, as the subject of their conversation had got close up to them.

"Good-day, Nelly; good-day, Michael," he said, putting out his hand. "You have got heavy loads; let me carry yours, Nelly."

She, however, declined his assistance.

"It is lighter than you suppose, and I can carry it well," she answered.

He looked somewhat angry and then walked on, Michael having to give way to let him pass. Instead, however, of doing so, he turned round suddenly and kept alongside Nelly, compelling Michael in consequence to walk behind them.

"I went to ask after your father, Nelly," he said, "and, hearing that you were away, came on to meet you. I am sorry to find he is no better."

"Thank you," said Nelly; "father is very ill, I fear; but God is merciful, and will take care of him and make him well if

He thinks fit."

Eban made no reply to this remark. He was not accustomed in his family to hear God spoken of except when that holy name was profaned by being joined to a curse.

"You had better let me take your creel, Nelly; it will be nothing to me."

"It is nothing to me either," answered Nelly, laughing. "I undertook to bring home the things, and I do not wish anybody else to do my work."

Still Eban persisted in his offers; she as constantly refusing, till they reached the top of the pathway.

"There," she said, "I have only to go down hill now, so you need not be afraid the load will break my back. Good-bye, Eban, you will be wanted at home I dare say."

Eban looked disconcerted; he appeared to have intended to accompany her down the hill, but he had sense enough to see that she did not wish him to do so. He stopped short, therefore.

"Good-bye, Eban," said Michael, as he passed him; "Nelly and I must get home as fast as we can to help granny nurse father."

"That's the work you are most fitted for," muttered Eban, as Michael went on. "If it was not for Nelly I should soon quarrel with that fellow. He is always talking about his duty, and fearing God, and such like things. If he had more spirit he would not hold back as he does from joining us. However, I will win him over some day when he is older, and it is not so easy to make a livelihood with his nets and lines alone as he supposes."

Eban remained on the top of the hill watching his young acquaintances as they descended the steep path, and then made his way homewards.

When Nelly and Michael arrived at the cottage the dame told them, to their sorrow, that their father was not better but rather worse. He still, however, forbad her sending for the doctor.

Day after day he continued much in the same state, though he endeavoured to encourage them with the hopes that he should get well at last.

The weather continued so bad all this time that Michael could not get out in the boat to fish with lines or lay down his lobster-pots. He and Nelly might have lost spirit had not their granny kept up hers and cheered them.

"We must expect bad times, my children, in this world," she said. "The sun does not always shine, but when clouds cover the sky we know they will blow away at last and we shall have fine days again. I have had many trials in my life, but here I am as well and hardy as ever. We cannot tell why some are spared and some are taken away. It is God's will, that's all we know. It was His will to take your parents, Michael, but He may think fit to let you live to a green old age. I knew your father and mother, and your grandmother too. Your grandmother had her trials, and heavy ones they were. I remember her a pretty, bright young woman as I ever saw. She lived in a gentleman's house as a sort of nurse or governess, where all were very fond of her, and she might have lived on in the house to the end of her days; but she was courted by a fine-looking fellow, who passed as the captain of a merchant vessel. A captain he was, though not of an honest trader, as he pretended, but of a smuggling craft, of which there were not a few in those days off this coast. The match was thought a good one for Nancy Trewinham when she married Captain Brewhard. They lived in good style and she was made much of, and looked upon as a lady, but before long she found out her husband's calling, and right-thinking and good as she was she could not enjoy her riches. She tried to persuade her husband to abandon his calling, but he laughed at her, and told her that if it was not for that he should be a beggar.

"He moved away from Penzance, where he had a house,

and after going to two or three other places, came to live near here. They had at this time two children, a fine lad of fifteen or sixteen years old, and your mother Judith.

"The captain was constantly away from home, and, to the grief of his wife, insisted on taking his boy with him. She well knew the hazardous work he was engaged in; so did most of the people on the coast, though he still passed where he lived for the master of a regular merchantman.

"There are some I have known engaged in smuggling for years, who have died quietly in their beds, but many, too, have been drowned at sea or killed in action with the king's cruisers, or shot landing their goods.

"There used to be some desperate work going on along this coast in my younger days.

"At last the captain, taking his boy with him, went away in his lugger, the 'Lively Nancy,' over to France. She was a fine craft, carrying eight guns, and a crew of thirty men or more. The king's cruisers had long been on the watch for her. As you know, smugglers always choose a dark and stormy night for running their cargoes. There was a cutter at the time off the coast commanded by an officer who had made up his mind to take the 'Lively Nancy,' let her fight ever so desperately. Her captain laughed at his threats, and declared that he would send her to the bottom first.

"I lived at that time with my husband and Nelly's mother, our only child, at Landewednach. It was blowing hard from the south-west with a cloudy sky, when just before daybreak a sound of firing at sea was heard. There were few people in the village who did not turn out to try and discover what was going on. The morning was dark, but we saw the flashes of guns to the westward, and my husband and others made out that there were two vessels engaged standing away towards Mount's Bay. We all guessed truly that one was the 'Lively Nancy,' and the other the king's cutter.

"Gradually the sounds of the guns grew less and the flashes seemed further off. After some time, however, they again drew near. It was evident that the cutter had attacked the lugger, which was probably endeavouring to get away out to sea or to round the Lizard, when, with a flowing sheet before the wind, she would have a better chance of escape.

"Just then daylight broke, and we could distinguish both the vessels close-hauled, the lugger to leeward trying to weather on the cutter, which was close to her on her quarter, both carrying as much sail as they could stagger under. They kept firing as fast as the guns could be loaded, each trying to knock away her opponent's spars, so that more damage was done to the rigging than to the crews of the vessels.

"The chief object of the smugglers was to escape, and this they hoped to do if they could bring down the cutter's mainsail. The king's officer knew that he should have the smugglers safe enough if he could but make them strike; this, however, knowing that they all fought with ropes round their necks, they had no thoughts of doing.

"Though the lugger stood on bravely, we could see that she was being jammed down gradually towards the shore. My good man cried out, 'that her fore-tack was shot away and it would now go hard with her.'

"The smugglers, however, in spite of the fire to which they were exposed, got it hauled down. The cutter was thereby enabled to range up alongside.

"By this time the two vessels got almost abreast of the point, but there were the Stags to be weathered. If the lugger could do that she might then keep away. There seemed a good chance that she would do it, and many hoped she would, for their hearts were with her rather than with the king's cruiser.

"She was not a quarter of a mile from the Stags when

down came her mainmast. It must have knocked over the man at the helm and injured others standing aft, for her head fell off and she ran on directly for the rocks. Still her crew did their best to save her. The wreck was cleared away, and once more she stood up as close as she could now be kept to the wind. One of her guns only was fired, for the crew had somewhat else to do just then. The cutter no longer kept as close to her as before; well did her commander know the danger of standing too near those terrible rocks, over which the sea was breaking in masses of foam.

"There seemed a chance that the lugger might still scrape clear of the rocks; if not, in a few moments she must be dashed to pieces and every soul on board perish.

"I could not help thinking of the poor lad whom his father had taken with him in spite of his mother's tears and entreaties. It must have been a terrible thought for the captain that he had thus brought his young son to an untimely end. For that reason I would have given much to see the lugger escape, but it was not to be.

"The seas came rolling in more heavily than before. A fierce blast struck her, and in another instant, covered with a shroud of foam, she was dashed against the wild rocks, and when we looked again she seemed to have melted away—not a plank of her still holding together.

"The cutter herself had but just weathered the rocks, and though she stood to leeward of them on the chance of picking up any of the luggers crew who might have escaped, not one was found.

"Such was the end of the 'Lively Nancy,' and your bold grandfather. Your poor grandmother never lifted up her head after she heard of what had happened. Still she struggled on for the sake of her little daughter, but by degrees all the money she possessed was spent. She at once moved into a small cottage, and then at last she and her young daughter found shelter in a single room. After this she did not live long, and your poor mother was left destitute. It was then your father met her, and though she had more education than he had, and remembered well the comfort she had once enjoyed, she consented to become his wife. He did his best for her, for he was a true-hearted, honest man, but she was ill fitted for the rough life a fisherman's wife has to lead, and when the news of her husband's death reached her she laid down and died.

"There, Michael, now you have learned all you are ever likely to know of your family, for no one can tell you more about them than I can.

"You see you cannot count upon many friends in the world except those you make yourself. But there is one Friend you have Who will never, if you trust to Him, leave or forsake you. He is truer than all earthly friends, and Paul Trefusis has acted a father's part in bringing you up to fear and honour Him."

"I do trust God, for it is He you speak of, granny," said Michael, "and I will try to love and obey Him as long as I live. He did what He knew to be best when He took my poor father away, and gave me such a good one as he who lies sick in there. I wish, granny, that you could have given me a better account of my grandfather."

"I thought it best that you should know the truth, Michael, and as you cannot be called to account for what he was, you need not trouble yourself about that matter. Your grandmother was an excellent woman, and I have a notion that she was of gentle blood, so it is well you should remember her name, and you may some day hear of her kith and kin: not that you are ever likely to gain anything by that; still it's a set-off against what your grandfather was, though people hereabouts will never throw that in your face."

"I should care little for what they may say," answered

Michael; "all I wish is to grow into a strong man to be able to work for you and Nelly and poor father, if he does not gain his strength. I will do my best now, and when the pilchard season comes on I hope, if I can get David Treloar or another hand in the boat, to do still better."

Chapter Four.

Day after day Paul Trefusis lay on his sick-bed. A doctor was sent for, but his report was unfavourable. Nelly asked him, with trembling lips, whether he thought her father would ever get well.

"You must not depend too much on that, my little maiden," he answered; "but I hope your brother, who seems an industrious lad, and that wonderful old woman, your grandmother, will help you to keep the pot boiling in the house, and I dare say you will find friends who will assist you when you require it. Good-bye; I'll come and see your father again soon; but all I can do is to relieve his pain."

Dame Lanreath and Michael did, indeed, do their best to keep the pot boiling: early and late Michael was at work, either digging in the garden, fishing in the harbour, or, when the weather would allow him, going with the boat outside. Young as he was, he was well able, under ordinary circumstances, to manage her by himself, though, of course, single-handed, he could not use the nets.

Though he toiled very hard, he could, however, obtain but a scanty supply of fish. When he obtained more than were required for home consumption, the dame would set off to dispose of them; but she had no longer the companionship of Nelly, who remained to watch over her poor father.

When Paul had strength sufficient to speak, which he had not always, he would give his daughter good advice, and warn her of the dangers to which she would be exposed in the world.

"Nelly," he said, "do not trust a person with a soft-speaking tongue, merely because he is soft-speaking; or one with good looks, merely because he has good looks. Learn his character first—how he spends his time, how he speaks about other people, and, more than all, how he speaks about God. Do not trust him because he says pleasant things to you. There is

Eban Cowan, for instance, a good-looking lad, with pleasant manners; but he comes of a bad stock, and is not brought up to fear God. It is wrong to speak ill of one's neighbours, so I have not talked of what I know about his father and his father's companions; but, Nelly dear, I tell you not to trust him or them till you have good cause to do so."

Nelly, like a wise girl, never forgot what her father said to her.

After this Paul grew worse. Often, for days together, he was racked with pain, and could scarcely utter a word. Nelly tended him with the most loving care. It grieved her tender heart to see him suffer; but she tried to conceal her sorrow, and he never uttered a word of complaint.

Michael had now become the main support of the family; for though Paul had managed to keep out of debt and have a small supply of money in hand, yet that was gradually diminishing.

"Never fear, Nelly," said Michael, when she told him one day how little they had left; "we must hope for a good pilchard-fishing, and we can manage to rub on till then. The nets are in good order, and I can get the help I spoke of; so that I can take father's place, and we shall have his share in the company's fishing."

Michael alluded to a custom which prevails among the fishermen on that coast. A certain number, who possess boats and nets, form a company, and fish together when the pilchards visit their coast, dividing afterwards the amount they receive for the fish caught.

"It is a long time to wait till then," observed Nelly.

"But on most days I can catch lobsters and crabs, and every time I have been out lately the fish come to my lines more readily than they used to do," answered Michael. "Do not be cast down, Nelly dear, we have a Friend in heaven, as father says,

Who will take care of us; let us trust Him."

Time passed on. Paul Trefusis, instead of getting better, became worse and worse. His once strong, stout frame was now reduced to a mere skeleton. Still Nelly and Michael buoyed themselves up with the hope that he would recover. Dame Lanreath knew too well that his days on earth were drawing to an end.

Michael had become the mainstay of the family. Whenever a boat could get outside, the "Wild Duck" was sure to be seen making her way towards the best fishing-ground.

Paul, before he started each day, inquired which way the wind was, and what sea there was on, and advised him where to go. "Michael," said Paul, as the boy came one morning to wish him good-bye, "fare thee well, lad; don't forget the advice I have given thee, and look after little Nelly and her grandmother, and may God bless and prosper thee;" and taking Michael's hand, Paul pressed it gently. He had no strength for a firm grasp now.

Michael was struck by his manner. Had it not been necessary to catch some fish he would not have left the cottage.

Putting the boat's sail and other gear on board, he pulled down the harbour. He had to pull some little way out to sea. The wind was setting on shore. He did not mind that, for he should sail back the faster. The weather did not look as promising as he could have wished: dark clouds were gathering to the north-west and passing rapidly over the sky. As he knew, should the wind stand, he could easily regain the harbour, he went rather more to the southward than he otherwise would have done, to a good spot, where he had often had a successful fishing. He had brought his dinner with him, as he intended to fish all day. His lines were scarcely overboard before he got a bite, and he was soon catching fish as fast as he could haul his lines on board. This put him in good spirits.

"Granny will have her creel full to sell to-morrow," he

thought. "Maybe I shall get back in time for her to set off today."

So eagerly occupied was he that he did not observe the change of the weather. The wind had veered round more to the northward. It was every instant blowing stronger and stronger, although, from its coming off the land, there was not much sea on.

At last he had caught a good supply of fish. By waiting he might have obtained many more, but he should then be too late for that day's market. Lifting his anchor, therefore, he got out his oars and began to pull homewards. The wind was very strong, and he soon found that, with all his efforts, he could make no headway. The tide, too, had turned, and was against him, sweeping round in a strong current to the southward. In vain he pulled. Though putting all the strength he possessed to his oars, still, as he looked at the shore, he was rather losing than gaining ground. He knew that the attempt to reach the harbour under sail would be hopeless; he should be sure to lose every tack he made. Already half a gale of wind was blowing, and the boat, with the little ballast there was in her, would scarcely look up even to the closest reefed canvas.

Again he dropped his anchor, intending to wait the turn of the tide, sorely regretting that he could not take the fish home in time for granny to sell on that day.

Dame Lanreath and Nelly had been anxiously expecting Michael's return, and the dame had got ready to set off as soon as he appeared with the fish they hoped he would catch. Still he did not come.

Paul had more than once inquired for him. He told Nelly to go out and see how the wind was, and whether there was much sea on.

Nelly made her way under the cliffs to the nearest point whence she could obtain a view of the mouth of the harbour and the sea beyond. She looked out eagerly for Michael's boat, hoping to discover her making her way towards the shore; but Nelly looked in vain. Already there was a good deal of sea on, and the wind, which had been blowing strong from the northwest, while she was standing there veered a point or two more to the northward.

"Where could Michael have gone?" She looked and looked till her eyes ached, still she could not bring herself to go back without being able to make some report about him. At last she determined to call at the cottage of Reuben Lanaherne, a friend of her father's, though a somewhat older man.

"What is it brings you here, my pretty maiden?" said Uncle Reuben, who, for a wonder, was at home, as Nelly, after gently knocking, lifted the latch and entered a room with sanded floor and blue painted ceiling.

"O Uncle Lanaherne," she said, "can you tell me where you think Michael has gone? he ought to have been back long ago."

"He would have been wiser not to have gone out at all with the weather threatening as it has been; but he is a handy lad in a boat, Nelly, and he will find his way in as well as any one, so don't you be unhappy about him," was the answer.

Still Reuben looked a little anxious, and putting on his hat, buttoning up his coat, and taking his glass under his arm, he accompanied Nelly to the point. He took a steady survey round.

"Michael's boat is nowhere near under sail," he observed. "There seems to me a boat, however, away to the southward, but, with the wind and tide as at present, she cannot be coming here. I wish I could make out more to cheer you, Nelly. You must tell your father that; and he knows if we can lend Michael a hand we will. How is he to-day?"

"He is very bad, Uncle Lanaherne," said Nelly, with a sigh; "I fear sometimes that he will never go fishing again."

"I am afraid not, Nelly," observed the rough fisherman, putting his hand on her head; "but you know you and your brother will always find a friend in Reuben Lanaherne. An honest man's children will never want, and if there ever was an honest man, your poor father is one. I will keep a look-out for Michael, but do not be cast down, Nelly; we shall see him before long."

The fisherman spoke in a cheery tone, but still he could not help feeling more anxiety than he expressed for Michael.

Every moment the wind was increasing, and the heavy seas which came rolling in showed that a gale had been blowing for some time outside.

Nelly hastened back to tell her father what Uncle Lanaherne had said.

When she got to his bedside she found that a great change had taken place during her absence. Her father turned his dim eye towards her as she entered, but had scarcely strength to speak, or beckon her with his hands. She bent over him.

"Nelly dear, where is Michael?" he asked, "I want to bless him, he must come quickly, for I have not long to stay."

"He has not come on shore yet, father, but Uncle Lanaherne is looking out for him," said Nelly.

"I wanted to see him again," whispered Paul. "It will be too late if he does not come now; so tell him, Nelly, that I do bless him, and I bless you, Nelly, bless you, bless you;" and his voice became fainter.

Nelly, seeing a change come over her father's features, cried out for her granny. Dame Lanreath hastened into the room. The old woman saw at a glance what had happened. Paul Trefusis was dead.

Closing his eyes, she took her grandchild by the hand, and led her out of the room.

Some time passed, however, before Nelly could realise

what had happened.

"Your father has gone, Nelly, but he has gone to heaven, and is happier far than he ever was or ever could be down on earth even in the best of times. Bad times may be coming, and God in His love and mercy took him that he might escape them."

"But, then, why didn't God take us?" asked Nelly, looking up. "I would have liked to die with him. Bad times will be as hard for us to bear as for him."

"God always does what is best, and He has a reason for keeping us on earth," answered the dame. "He has kept me well-nigh fourscore years, and given me health and strength, and good courage to bear whatever I have had to bear, and He will give you strength, Nelly, according to your need."

"Ah, I was wicked to say what I did," answered Nelly; "but I am sad about father and you and myself, and very sad, too, about Michael. He will grieve so when he comes home and finds father gone, if he comes at all. And, O granny, I begin to fear that he won't come home! what has happened to him I cannot tell; and if you had seen the heavy sea there was rolling outside you would fear the worst."

"Still, Nelly, we must trust in God; if He has taken Michael, He has done it for the best, not the worst, Nelly," answered Dame Lanreath. "But when I say this, Nelly, I don't want to stop your tears, they are given in mercy to relieve your grief; but pray to God, Nelly, to help us; He will do so—only trust Him."

Chapter Five.

The day was drawing to a close when the storm, which had been threatening all the morning on which Paul Trefusis died, swept fiercely up the harbour, showing that the wind had again shifted to the westward.

Poor Nelly, though cast down with grief at her father's death, could not help trembling as she thought of Michael, exposed as she knew he must be to its rage. Was he, too, to be taken away from them?

She was left much alone, as Dame Lanreath had been engaged, with the assistance of a neighbour, in the sad duty of laying out the dead man. Nelly several times had run out to look down the harbour, hoping against hope that she might see Michael's boat sailing up it.

At length, in spite of the gale, she made her way to Reuben Lanaherne's cottage. His wife and daughter were seated at their work, but he was not there. Agitated and breathless from encountering the fierce wind, she could scarcely speak as she entered.

"Sit down, maiden; what ails thee?" said Dame Lanaherne, rising, and kindly placing her on a stool by her side.

Nelly could only answer with sobs.

Just then old Reuben himself entered, shaking the spray from his thick coat.

"How is thy father, Nelly?" he asked.

"He has gone," she answered, sobbing afresh. "And, O Uncle Reuben, have you seen Michael's boat? can you tell me where he is?"

"I have not forgotten him, Nelly, and have been along the shore as far as I could make my way on the chance that he might have missed the harbour, and had run for Kynance Cove, but not a sign of him or his boat could I see. I wish I had better news for you, Nelly. And your good father gone too! Don't take on so—

he is free from pain now—happy in heaven; and there is One above Who will look after Michael, though what has become of him is more than I can tell you."

The old fisherman's words brought little comfort to poor Nelly, though he and his wife and daughter did their best to console her. They pressed her to remain with them, but she would not be absent longer from her granny, and, thanking them for their kindness, hurried homewards.

The wind blew fiercely, but no rain had as yet fallen.

Their neighbour, having rendered all the assistance required, had gone away, and the old dame and her young grandchild sat together side by side in the outer room. They could talk only of Michael. The dame did not dare to utter what she thought. His small boat might have been swamped in the heavy sea, or he might have fallen overboard and been unable to regain her; or, attempting to land on a rocky coast, she might have been dashed to pieces, and he swept off by the receding surf. Such had been the fate of many she had known.

As each succeeding gust swept by, poor Nelly started and trembled in spite of her efforts to keep calm.

At length down came the rain battering against the small panes of glass.

At that instant there was a knocking at the door.

"Can you give us shelter from the storm, good folks?" said a voice; and, the latch being lifted, an elderly gentleman, accompanied by two ladies, one of whom was young and the other more advanced in life, appeared at the entrance.

They evidently took it for granted that they should not be denied.

"You are welcome, though you come to a house of mourning," said Dame Lanreath, rising, while Nelly hastened to place stools for them to sit on.

"I am afraid, then, that we are intruders," said the

gentleman, "and we would offer to go on, but my wife and daughter would be wet through before we could reach any other shelter."

"We would not turn any one away, especially you and Mistress Tremayne," said the dame, looking at the elder lady.

"What! do you know us?" asked the gentleman.

"I know Mistress Tremayne and the young lady from her likeness to what I recollect of her mother," answered Dame Lanreath. "I seldom forget a person I once knew, and she has often bought fish of me in days gone by."

"And I, too, recollect you. If I mistake not you used to be pretty widely known as Polly Lanreath," said the lady, looking at the old fish-wife.

"And so I am now, Mistress Tremayne," answered the dame, "though not known so far and wide as I once was. I can still walk my twenty miles a-day; but years grow on one; and when I see so many whom I have known as children taken away, I cannot expect to remain hale and strong much longer."

"You have altered but little since I knew you," observed Mrs Tremayne, "and I hope that you may retain your health and strength for many years to come."

"That's as God wills," said the dame. "I pray it may be so for the sake of my little Nelly here."

"She is your grandchild, I suppose," observed Mrs Tremayne.

"Ay, and the only one I have got to live for now. Her father has just gone, and she and I are left alone."

"O granny, but there is Michael; don't talk of him as gone," exclaimed Nelly. "He will come back, surely he will come back."

This remark of Nelly's caused Mr and Mrs Tremayne to make further inquiries.

They at first regretted that they had been compelled to

take shelter in the cottage, but as the dame continued talking, their interest in what she said increased.

"It seemed strange, Mistress Tremayne, that you should have come here at this moment," she observed. "Our Michael is the grandson of one whom you knew well in your childhood; she was Nancy Trewinham, who was nurse in the family of your mother, Lady Saint Mabyn; and you, if I mistake not, were old enough at the time to remember her."

"Yes, indeed, I do perfectly well; and I have often heard my mother express her regret that so good and gentle a young woman should have married a man who, though apparently well-to-do in the world, was more than suspected to be of indifferent character," said the lady. "We could gain no intelligence of her after she left Penzance, though I remember my father saying that he had no doubt a noted smuggler whose vessel was lost off this coast was the man she had married. Being interested in her family, he made inquiries, but could not ascertain whether she had survived her unhappy husband or not. And have you, indeed, taken charge of her grandson in addition to those of your own family whom you have had to support?"

"It was not I took charge of the boy, but my good son-in-law, who lies dead there," said the dame. "He thought it but a slight thing, and only did what he knew others would do by him."

"He deserved not the less credit," said Mr Tremayne. "We shall, indeed, be anxious to hear that the boy has come to no harm, and I am sure that Mrs Tremayne will be glad to do anything in her power to assist you and him should he, as I hope, have escaped. We purpose staying at Landewednach for a few days to visit the scenery on the coast, and will send down to inquire to-morrow."

While Mr and Mrs Tremayne and the old dame had been talking, Miss Tremayne had beckoned to Nelly to come and sit by her, and, speaking in a kind and gentle voice, had tried to comfort the young girl. She, however, could only express her hope that Michael had by some means or other escaped. Though Nelly knew that that hope was vain, the sympathy which was shown her soothed her sorrow more than the words which were uttered.

Sympathy, in truth, is the only balm that one human being can pour into the wounded heart of another. Would that we could remember that in all our grief and sufferings we have One in heaven Who can sympathise with us as He did when He wept with the sorrowing family at Bethany.

The rain ceased almost as suddenly as it had commenced, and as Mr and Mrs Tremayne, who had left their carriage on the top of the hill, were anxious to proceed on their journey, they bade Dame Lanreath and Nelly good-bye, again apologising for having intruded on them.

"Don't talk of that please, Mistress Tremayne," said the old dame. "Your visit has been a blessing to us, as it has taken us off our own sad thoughts. Nelly already looks less cast down, from what the young lady has been saying to her, and though you can't bring the dead to life we feel your kindness."

"You will let me make it rather more substantial, then, by accepting this trifle, which may be useful under the present circumstances," said the gentleman, offering a couple of guineas.

The old dame looked at them, a struggle seemed to be going on within her.

"I thank you kindly, sir, that I do," she answered; "but since my earliest days I have gained my daily bread and never taken charity from any one."

"But you must not consider this as charity, dame," observed Mrs Tremayne; "it is given to show our interest in your little granddaughter and in the boy whom your son-in-law and you have so generously protected so many years. I should, indeed, feel bound to assist him, and therefore on his account pray receive it and spend it as you may require."

The dame's scruples were at length overcome, and her guests, after she had again expressed her feelings of gratitude, took their departure.

They had scarcely gone when Eban Cowan appeared at the door.

"I have just heard what has happened, and I could not let the day pass without coming to tell you how sorry I am," he said, as he entered.

Nelly thanked him warmly.

"Father has gone to heaven and is at rest," she said, quietly.

"I should think that you would rather have had him with you down on earth," observed Eban, who little comprehended her feelings.

"So I would, but it was God's will to take him, and he taught me to say, 'Thy will be done;' and I can say that though I grieve for his loss," answered Nelly. "But, O Eban, when you came I thought that you had brought some tidings of Michael."

"No! Where is he? I did not know that he was not at home."

Nelly then told Eban how Michael had gone away with the boat in the morning and had not returned. "I will go and search for him then," he said. "He has run in somewhere, perhaps, along the coast. I wonder, when you spoke to Uncle Lanaherne, that he did not set off at once. But I will go. I'll get father to send some men with me with ropes, and if he is alive and clinging to a rock, as he may be, we will bring him back."

Nelly poured out her thanks to Eban, who, observing that there was no time to be lost, set off to carry out his proposal.

Dame Lanreath had said but little. She shook her head when he had gone, as Nelly continued praising him.

"He is brave and bold, Nelly, but that could be said of Captain Brewhard and many others I have known, who were bad husbands and false friends, and there is something about the lad I have never liked. He is inclined to be friendly now; and as you grow up he will wish, maybe, to be more friendly; but I warn you against him, Nelly dear. Though he speaks to you ever go fair, don't trust him."

"But I must be grateful to him as long as I live if he finds Michael," answered Nelly, who thought her grandmother condemned Eban without sufficient cause.

Had she known how he had often talked to Michael, she might have been of a different opinion.

The storm continued to blow as fiercely as ever, and the rain again came pelting down; ever and anon peals of thunder rattled and crashed overhead, and flashes of lightning, seen more vividly through the thickening gloom, darted from the sky.

Dame Lanreath and Nelly sat in their cottage by the dead —the old woman calm and unmoved, though Nelly, at each successive crash of thunder or flash of lightning, drew closer to her grandmother, feeling more secure in the embrace of the only being on whom she had now to rely for protection in the wide world.

Chapter Six.

Young Michael sat all alone in his boat, tossed about by the foaming seas. His anchor held, so there was no fear of his drifting. But that was not the only danger to which he was exposed. At any moment a sea might break on board and wash him away, or swamp the boat.

He looked round him, calmly considering what was best to be done. No coward fear troubled his mind, yet he clearly saw the various risks he must run. He thought of heaving his ballast overboard and trying to ride out the gale where he was, but then he must abandon all hope of reaching the harbour by his own unaided efforts. He might lash himself to a thwart, and thus escape being washed away; still the fierce waves might tear the boat herself to pieces, so that he quickly gave up that idea. He was too far off to be seen from the shore, except perhaps by the keen-sighted coast-guard men; but even if seen, what boat would venture out into the fast-rising sea to his rescue. He must, he felt, depend upon himself, with God's aid, for saving his life.

Any longer delay would only increase his peril. The wind and tide would prevent him gaining any part of the coast to the northward. He would therefore make sail and run for Landewednach, for not another spot where he had the slightest prospect of landing in safety was to be found between the Gull Rock and the beach at that place. He very well knew, indeed, the danger he must encounter even there, but it was a choice of evils. He quickly made up his mind.

He at first set to work to bail out the boat, for already she had shipped a good deal of water. He had plenty of sea room, so that he might venture to lift his anchor. But it was no easy work, and the sea, which broke over the bows again and again, made him almost relinquish the effort, and cut the cable instead. Still he knew the importance of having his anchor ready to drop, should he be unable to beach the boat on his arrival at the spot he had selected, so again he tried, and up it came. He quickly hauled it in, and running up his sail he sprang to the tiller, hauling aft his main-sheet.

Away flew the boat amid the tumbling seas, which came rolling in from the westward. He held the sheet in his hand, for there was now as much wind as the boat could look up to, and a sudden blast might at any moment send her over. That, too, Michael knew right well. On she flew like a sea-bird amid the foaming waves, now lifted to the summit of one, now dropping down into the hollow, each sea as it came hissing up threatening to break on board; now he kept away to receive its force on his quarter; now he again kept his course.

The huge Gull Rock rose up under his lee, the breakers dashing furiously against its base; then Kynance Cove, with its fantastically-shaped cliffs, opened out, but the sea roared and foamed at their base, and not a spot of sand could he discover on which he could hope to beach his boat, even should he pass through the raging surf unharmed. Meantale Point, Pradanack, and the Soapy Rock appeared in succession, but all threatened him alike with destruction should he venture near them.

He came abreast of a little harbour, but he had never been in there, and numerous rocks, some beneath the surface, others rising but just above it, lay off its entrance, and the risk of running for it he considered was too great to be encountered. Those on shore might have seen his boat as she flew by, but, should they have done so, even the bravest might have been unwilling to risk their lives on the chance of overtaking her before she met that fate to which they might well have believed she was doomed.

Michael cast but a glance or two to ascertain whether any one was coming; he had little expectation of assistance, but still his courage did not fail him.

The rocks were passed; he could already distinguish over

his bow the lighthouses on the summit of the Lizard Point. Again he kept away and neared the outer edge of a line of breakers which roared fiercely upon it. He must land there notwithstanding, or be lost, for he knew that his boat could not live going through the race to the southward of the Lizard.

When off the Stags he could distinguish people moving along the shore. He had been seen by them he knew, and perhaps a boat might be launched and come to his rescue. There was no time, however, for consideration. What he had to do must be promptly done.

The water in the bay was somewhat smoother than it had hitherto been. In a moment his sail was lowered and his anchor let go. The rain came down heavily.

"The wind is falling," he thought; "I will wait till the turn of the tide, when, perhaps, there will be less surf on."

He could see the people on the shore watching him, but no attempt was made to launch a boat; indeed he knew that no boat could pass that foaming barrier in safety. He sat down with folded arms, waiting the progress of events. His mind was occupied for a time rather with those at home than about himself; he thought of little Nelly and of Dame Lanreath, and of the kind friend of his youth who had, though he knew it not at that time, left this world of toil and trouble. He had a simple faith in the merits of One Who had died for him, and he had perfect trust, not in his own honesty and uprightness, but in the merits and all-sufficient atonement of that loving Saviour Who died for him. He could therefore, young as he was, calmly contemplate the probability of being unable after all to reach the shore. Still he would not allow himself to dwell long on that matter.

He was soon aroused indeed to exertion by finding the seas breaking into his boat. He bailed away as fast as they came on board. But he saw that he must abandon all hope of remaining where he was. Should he stay much longer the boat might be swamped; the surf, too, might increase, and more effectually than at present bar his progress to the shore. Another huge sea rolling in half filled his boat. Undaunted, he bailed it out. A second of like size might sink her.

Evening was coming on; he must dare the fearful passage through the breakers, or perish where he was. He stood up, holding on to the mast, that he might survey the shore. He was abreast of the best place for landing, although he was convinced there were rocks to the north and south of him, their black heads appearing every now and then amid the snow-white foam. In a moment, should his boat touch them, they would dash her to fragments.

Promptly Michael made up his mind what to do. Hoisting his foresail he carried the main-sheet aft, and felt that the tiller was securely fixed. Taking out his knife, he held it in his teeth— he had sharpened it afresh the previous evening. With one hand holding the main halyards, with a stroke he severed the cable, then as the boat paid off up went his mainsail and he sprang aft to the helm. The sheet was eased off. The hissing seas followed fast astern. In another minute he would be among the raging breakers, and then safe on shore, or, what was too probable, whirled and tossed and tumbled over and over as he and the fragments of his boat were carried back in their cruel embrace.

Mr and Mrs Tremayne and their daughter had reached the little hotel at the Lizard Head, when they heard that a small boat had been seen in a fearfully perilous position anchored at a short distance outside the breakers. They hastened down to the beach, where some of the coast-guard men and several other persons were collected.

They made inquiries as to the probability of the boat reaching the shore in safety.

"Not the slightest hope through such a surf as this," was

the answer.

"Who is on board?" asked Mr Tremayne.

"It seems to be a young lad, as far as we can make out," said a coast-guard man. "His best chance is to hold on till low water, when, as there will be a pretty broad piece of sand, if the wind goes down, he may happen to get in without being swamped."

"But if the wind does not go down, and the weather still looks threatening, what can he do?"

"His fate will be that of many another poor fellow," said the man. "He is a brave young chap, though, or he would not have brought up in the way he did. I have not once seen him waving his arms or seeming to be crying out for help, as most would be."

"Can he be young Michael Penguyne, of whom we have just heard!" exclaimed Mrs Tremayne. "Oh, can nothing be done to save him?"

"Will none of you fine fellows launch a boat and go out and try and bring in the boy?" asked Mr Tremayne. "I will give twenty pounds to the crew of the boat which brings him in."

"I am sorry, sir, that I cannot allow my men to go out," said the officer of the coast-guard, who heard the offer made. "We should not have waited for a reward if it could be done, but the best boat we have would be swamped to a certainty, and the lives of all her crew sacrificed. I much regret being compelled to say this; there is not a man here who would not do his best to save the life of the lad if it were possible."

"Are none of the fishermen's boats better fitted for the purpose?" asked Mr Tremayne. "I will give twenty-five pounds to the boat which saves the lad. Surely if so small a boat as his can live, a large fishing-boat would run but comparatively little risk."

The officer explained that the danger would be incurred

in passing through the breakers, and that once outside, although the sea was very heavy, a boat properly handled would keep afloat.

"I have," he added, "sent to a little harbour to the north of this, but the boats there are small, and I doubt whether any of the fishermen will venture so near the breakers as that boat has brought up. I will, however, send again with your generous offer, though some time must elapse before a boat can be got ready, even if a crew can be found willing to risk their lives in the service."

"I will go myself to urge them to undertake it if you can devise no other means of saving the lad," said Mr Tremayne.

"The distance is considerable, and it will be night before you can reach the place," answered the officer. "I would advise you, sir, not to make the attempt. They will trust to my promise, as I will send one of my own men."

"Tell them you will give them twenty-five pounds if they will start at once," exclaimed Mrs Tremayne, eagerly; "surely men will not stand calmly by and allow the poor boy to perish in their sight."

"I will do as you wish," answered the officer.

Just as they were speaking, however, there was a cry from those looking on.

"He has cut his cable—he has hoisted his sail—he is going to venture it," exclaimed several people simultaneously.

The boat's head was turned towards the shore. Onward she came. Now she rose to the summit of a huge wave, now plunged downwards. For an instant the sail flapped, becalmed by another sea which rolled up astern.

A cry escaped the spectators: "She will be swamped! she will be swamped!"

But no; again the sail filled and on she came. The young boy was seen seated in the stern of his boat grasping the tiller with one hand and the main-sheet with the other. Over she heeled to the blast—again she rose, and again sunk down, and now she was among the hissing, roaring, foaming breakers. The waters bubbled up, tumbling into her on either side; but still the boy held firm hold of his tiller. Again the sail flapped—there was a sudden lull.

"She is lost, she is lost!" was the cry. "The next sea must swamp her;" but the wind came faster than the wave—the sail bulged out, and on she flew.

For another moment she seemed to hang in the midst of a breaker as it rushed backwards from the shore, but another lifted her, and, carried forward on its crest, she came like a thing of life escaping from her savage pursuers towards the beach.

A dozen stout hands, incited by the address of Mr Tremayne, rushed forward to grasp the boat, regardless now of their own safety, for the work was one of no little danger; ere they could seize the boat's gunwale she might be dashed against them, or be swept out by the receding wave as it went hissing backwards in a sheet of foam. But they were well accustomed to the duty they had undertaken.

Michael to the last kept his seat, steering his boat stem on to the beach. As he felt the keel touch the sand he sprang forward and was grasped by the sturdy arms of one of those who had gone to his rescue, and carried in triumph out of the reach of the foaming breaker, which came roaring up as if fierce at the escape of its prey.

With difficulty those who had gone down to seize the boat made their way after their companion, and she, before they could haul her up, was thrown on the beach and rolled over and over with her sides crushed in.

"Oh, the boat, the boat! what will poor father and those at home do?" exclaimed Michael, as he saw what had happened. "I thought to have saved her."

"Never mind the boat," answered a stout lad, one of those who had gone down to his rescue, wringing him by the hand. "We are right glad to have you safe. I only got here just in time to see you standing for the shore. I did not think you would reach it. I have been hunting for you all along the coast, and made sure that you were lost."

"Thank you, Eban," answered Michael, for it was Eban Cowan who spoke to him. "But poor father will grieve when he hears the boat is lost after all."

"Thy father won't grieve for that or anything else, Michael," said Eban, thoughtlessly; "he is dead."

"Dead!" exclaimed poor Michael, grasping the arm of the man who had brought him on shore, and who was still standing by him, and overcome by the strain on his nerves, which he had hitherto so manfully endured, and the sad news so abruptly given him, he would have fallen to the ground had not the fisherman supported him.

Mr Tremayne and his wife and daughter now came up.

"Poor boy, it is not surprising that he should give way at last," observed Mrs Tremayne. "We will have him carried to our inn, where he can be properly attended to."

Mr Tremayne agreed to her proposal, and, begging two of the stout fishermen to carry the lad, he promised a reward to those who could secure the boat and her gear.

"That will be my charge," said the coast-guard officer. "But I am afraid that the boat herself is a complete wreck, and that very little of her gear will be saved."

Michael, on being placed in a comfortable bed in the inn, soon returned to consciousness, and was greatly surprised to find two kind-looking ladies watching by his side. The younger one called her father from an adjoining room.

"You have had a hard tussle for your life; you behaved courageously, my lad," observed Mr Tremayne, taking his hand.

"I am thankful that God has spared my life," answered Michael in a low voice, which showed how much his strength was prostrated. "But, O sir, Eban told me that father is dead, and the boat is all knocked to pieces, and what will Nelly and poor granny do? Next to God, they can only look to the boat and me for help."

"What! young as you are, do you expect to be able to support yourself and those you speak of?" asked Mrs Tremayne.

"Yes; father gave them into my charge, and if God had given me strength, and the boat had been spared, I would have done my best."

"We know Nelly and your granny, and more about you than you may suppose," said Mrs Tremayne, kindly; "we paid them a visit to-day, and heard of their loss. But set your mind at rest about your boat, we will endeavour to obtain another for you, and help you in any other way you may wish."

Michael expressed his gratitude with an overflowing heart. A night's quiet rest completely restored his strength, and, being eager to assure Nelly and Dame Lanreath of his safety, after he had bade his new friends good-bye he set off on his return home.

Mrs Tremayne promised to have his boat looked after, and to pay him a visit in the course of a day or two to arrange about the purchase of another.

On reaching home Michael found that Eban Cowan had been before him, and given Nelly and her granny tidings of his safety. They had heard, however, only of the loss of his boat, and had been naturally anxious at the thoughts of what they should do without her. The news he brought that he was to have a new one greatly revived their spirits.

"God is indeed kind to us in sending us help in our time of need," said Dame Lanreath. "O my children! never forget His loving-kindness, but serve and obey Him as long as you live."

Michael's grief was renewed as he went in to see the friend who had acted the part of a father to him all his life; but happily deep grief does not endure long in young hearts, and he now looked forward to Mr Tremayne's promised visit.

"I hope the young lady and her mother will come with him. O Nelly! she looked like an angel as she watched by me, when I scarcely knew whether I was alive or being knocked over and over in the breakers," he observed. "For hours after I was safe on shore I had their sound in my ears in a way I never knew before."

Mr Tremayne came to the cottage just as Dame Lanreath, with Michael and Nelly, had returned from attending the funeral of Paul Trefusis. It was a calm and lovely day, and contrasted greatly with the weather which had before prevailed.

In the harbour, just below the cottage, lay a boat somewhat smaller than the "Wild Duck," but nearly new, with freshly-tanned sails, and well fitted in every respect. Mrs and Miss Tremayne were seated in it, with two men who had rowed it round from the Lizard.

Mr Tremayne invited the inmates of the cottage to come down and see it.

"What do you think of her?" he asked, after they had greeted the two ladies.

"She is a handy craft, sir, and just suited for this place," answered Michael.

"I hope you will find her so," replied Mr Tremayne. "Here is a paper which assigns her to you as her master, and if you will moor her fast her present crew will leave her, as we purpose to continue our journey by land, and have ordered the carriage to meet us at the top of the hill."

Michael was unable to express his gratitude in words. Dame Lanreath spoke for him.

"May God reward you and your wife and children for

your kindness to the orphans, and to an old woman who has well-nigh run her course on earth. We were cast down, though we know that His mercy endureth for ever, and you have lifted us up and shown us that He is faithful and never fails to send help in time of need."

Nelly took Miss Tremayne's hand, and, prompted by her feelings, kissed it affectionately; but even she was for the moment unable to express her feelings by words.

"Thank you, sir, thank you," said Michael at last, as they went back. "You have made a man of me, and I can now work for those who have to look to me for support."

"I hope you will have the strength, as I am sure you have the will, and may God bless you, my lad," said Mr Tremayne, shaking him warmly by the hand, for he was far more pleased with the few words Michael had uttered than had he poured out his gratitude in measured language. As he and the ladies proceeded up the pathway, Nelly ran into the cottage. She soon again overtook them.

"Will you please, miss, take these small shells?" she said; "they are little worth, I fear, but I have nothing else to give which you might wish to accept, and they may put you in mind of this place, and those who will pray for you and bless your father and mother as long as they live."

Miss Tremayne, much pleased, thanked Nelly for her gift, and, assuring her that she should never forget her or Michael and her granny, accepted the gift.

It is scarcely necessary to say that Michael spent a considerable portion of the remainder of the day examining his new boat over and over again, blessing the donor in his heart, and thankful that he should now be able to support Nelly and her granny.

Then the little family assembled in their sitting room, and offered up their thanks to the merciful Being Who looked down upon them in their distress.

Chapter Seven.

Michael Penguyne made ample use of his new boat. Nelly proposed that she should be called the "Dove."

"You see she was sent to us when all around seemed so dark and gloomy, just as the dove returned to Noah, to show that God had not forgotten him."

"Then we will call her the 'Dove'," said Michael; and the "Dove" from henceforth became the name of Michael's new boat.

Early and late Michael was in his boat, though he took good care not to be caught to leeward of his port again by a gale of wind. When ashore he was employed mending his nets and refitting his boat's gear or his fishing-lines. Never for a moment was he idle, for he always found something which ought to be done; each rope's-end was pointed; his rigging was never chafed; and the moment any service was wanted he put it on.

Thus a couple of years passed by, Dame Lanreath and Nelly setting out day after day to sell the fish or lobsters and crabs he caught, for which they seldom failed to obtain a good price.

At length, however, he found that he could do better with a mate.

"I must get David Treloar, as I said some time ago," he observed to Nelly. "He is twice as strong as I am, though it would not do to trust him alone in a boat, as he never seems to know which way the wind is, or how the tide is running; but he is honest and good-natured, and staunch as steel, and he will do what I tell him. That's all I want. If he had been with me in the little 'Duck,' we might have gained the harbour and saved her, and though I take all the care I can, yet I may be caught again in the same way."

David Treloar was a nephew of old Reuben Lanaherne, who had done his best to bring up the poor lad, and make a fisherman of him. His father had been lost at sea, and his mother had gone out of her mind, and soon afterwards died.

Michael found him near his uncle's house, attempting, though not very expertly, to mend a net.

He was a broad-shouldered, heavy-looking youth, with an expression of countenance which at first sight appeared far from prepossessing; but when spoken to kindly, or told to do anything he liked—and he was ready to do most things—it brightened up, and even a stranger would have said he was a trustworthy fellow, though he might be lacking in intelligence.

"So glad you are come, Michael," he said. "Here have I been working away at these meshes, and cannot make them come even; the more I pull at them the worse they are. Just do you use your fingers and settle the job for me, and I will do anything for you."

"I know you will, David, and so I am pretty certain that you will come and work in my boat."

"What, this afternoon?" asked David.

"No, but always. I want you to be my mate."

"Hurra! hurra! that I will, lad, with all my heart. Uncle Reuben has got enough lads of his own, he does not want me, and the rest are always making fun at me; but you won't do that, Michael, I know. We will soon show them that we can catch as many fish as they can, you and I together; and uncle often says I am as strong as a grown man, and stronger than many." And the young Hercules stretched out his brawny arms.

Michael had not expected to obtain a mate so easily, for David never thought of making terms; provided he got food enough for the day, that was all he thought about. Michael, however, intended to settle that matter with Uncle Reuben. His wish was to act justly towards all men, and pay David fully as much as he was worth.

Able now to use his nets, Michael could look forward to

the pilchard season, when he might hope to reap a rich harvest from the sea.

Soon after this he fell in with Eban Cowan.

"So I see you have got that dolt David Treloar as your mate," observed Eban. "If you had asked me, I would have advised you to take a chap worth two of him. He is big and strong enough, but he has no sense. I wonder, indeed, Michael, that you can go on year after year content to catch a few fish and lobsters, when you might make no end of money and live at home most days in the week enjoying your comfort and doing nothing. Just see how father and I live. You don't suppose the mill, and the fish, and our few acres of ground enable us to do that."

"I don't ask how you get your living—I do not wish to interfere with my neighbours; but I know that it is my duty to work hard every day that the weather will let me," answered Michael.

"That may be your taste; but I wonder you like to see Nelly wearing her old frock and hood which have become far too small for her, and Aunt Lanreath's old jacket and petticoat are well-nigh worn out."

Michael acknowledged that such was the case, and observed that he hoped they would soon get new garments.

"You might get them at once if you will join us in our business," answered Eban. "What with the fellows who have gone to sea, and some few who have been taken and sent to prison, and those who have been drowned or lost their lives in other ways, we have not as many men as we want. There is good pay to be got, and other profits besides. You would be perfectly safe, for you have a good character, and no one would suspect you of being engaged in the free-trade service."

"I tell you, Eban, once for all, I will have nothing to do with smuggling," answered Michael, firmly. "You say no one will suspect me, but you forget that God sees and hears everything we do, or say, or think. Though my fellow-men might not suspect me, He would know that I was engaged in unlawful work. Darkness is no darkness to Him. Day and night to Him are both alike."

"I don't let myself think about those sort of things," answered Eban Cowan, in an angry tone. "I ask you again, will you be a sensible fellow and unite with us as I have invited you?"

"No, I will not," said Michael. "I do not wish to be unfriendly with you, but when you ask me to do what I know to be wrong I cannot look upon you as a friend."

"Take your own way, then," exclaimed Eban, angrily. "You may think better of the matter by-and-by: then all you have to do is to come to me and say so."

Eban and Michael parted for the time. The former, however, was a constant visitor at Dame Lanreath's cottage. He did not disguise his admiration for Nelly Trefusis. She might have been flattered, for he was a good-looking, fair-spoken youth, and as he dressed well and had always plenty of money in his pocket, he was looked upon as one of the principal young men in the neighbourhood.

Still Nelly did not consider him equal to Michael.

Time went on: she was becoming a young woman, and Michael was no longer the little boy she had looked upon in her early days as her brother. He, too, had ceased to treat her with the affectionate familiarity he used to do when he supposed her to be his sister. Still he looked upon her as the being of all others whom he was bound to love, and protect, and support to the utmost of his power. Had, however, any young man whom he esteemed, and whom Nelly liked, appeared and offered to become her husband, he would possibly have advised her to accept him, though he might have felt that the light of his home had departed. Indeed, he was so occupied that the thought of marrying at some future time had never entered his head.

Though Nelly gave Eban Cowan no encouragement, he still continued, whenever he could get a fair pretence, to visit the cottage, and never failed to walk by her side when he met her out. Generally he came saying that he wished to see Michael, whom he always spoke of as his most intimate friend, though Michael did not consider himself so. He knew too much about Eban to desire his friendship; indeed, he doubted very much that Eban really cared for him.

"Your friend Eban has been here again to-day," said Nelly, one evening when Michael returned home late. "He waited and waited, and though I told him I could not say when you would come back, he still sat on, declaring that he must see you, as he wanted you to go somewhere with him, or do something, though what it was he would not tell us. At last, as it grew dark, he was obliged to be off, and neither granny nor I invited him to stay longer."

"I am glad he did go," answered Michael; "but do not call him my friend. If he was a true friend he would give me good advice and try to lead me aright; instead of that he gives me bad advice, and tries to lead me to do what I know is wrong. There — you now know what I think of Eban Cowan."

"And you think very rightly," observed Dame Lanreath. "I do not trust him, and perhaps you know more about him and have greater reasons for not liking him than I have."

"Michael," said Nelly, looking up, "I will trust only those whom you trust, and I do not wish to like any one whom you do not like."

Still, although Nelly took no care to show any preference for Eban, it was not in her heart to be rude or unkind to him; but Dame Lanreath tried to make him understand that his visits were not wished for. He, however, fancied that she alone did not like him, and still flattered himself that he was making his way with

Nelly.

Thus matters went on month after month. Michael and David Treloar succeeded together better even than at first expected. David was always ready to do the hard work, and, placing perfect confidence in Michael's skill and judgment, readily obeyed him.

It was the height of summer-time. The pilchards in vast schools began to visit the coast of Cornwall, and the fishermen in all directions were preparing for their capture. The boats were got ready, the nets thoroughly repaired, and corks and leads and tow lines and warps fitted. *Huers*, as the men are called who watch for the fish, had taken their stations on every height on the look-out for their approach. Each *huer* kept near him the "white bush," which is the name given to a mass of furze covered with tow or white ribbons. This being raised aloft is the sign that a school is in sight. The boats employed were of two descriptions, the largest of from twenty to thirty tons, carrying seven or eight men; and the smaller somewhat larger than the "Dove," having only three or four men.

Michael had succeeded in obtaining another hand, so that, small as his boat was, he was fully able to take a part in the work.

The pilchard belongs to the herring family, but is somewhat smaller, and differs from that fish in external appearance, having a shorter head and a more compact body; its scales, too, are rather longer than those of the common herring. It is supposed to retire during the winter to the deep water of the ocean, and to rise only as the summer approaches to the surface, when it commences its travels and moves eastward towards the English Channel.

At first it forms only small bands, but these increase till a large army is collected, under the guidance, it is supposed, of a chief. Onward it makes its way, pursued by birds of prey who pounce down and carry off thousands of individuals, whose loss, however, scarcely diminishes the size of the mighty host. Voracious fish, too, pursue the army as it advances in close columns, and swallow immense numbers.

As it approaches the Land's End it divides, one portion making its way northward along the west coast, while the other moves forward along the south coast towards the Start.

The huers can distinguish the approach of a school by a change in the colour of the sea. As it draws near, the water appears to leap and boil like a cauldron, while at night the ocean is spread over, as it were, with a sheet of liquid light, brilliant as when the moonbeams play on the surface rippled by a gentle breeze.

From early dawn a number of boats had been waiting off the shore, keeping their position by an occasional pull at the oars as necessity required, with their nets ready to cast at a moment's warning. Michael's boat was among them. He and his companions cast their eyes constantly at the huers on the summit of the cliffs above, anxiously expecting the signal that a school had been seen in the far distance. But whether it would approach the shore near enough to enable them to encircle it was uncertain. It might come towards them, but then it might suddenly sweep round to a different part of the coast or dart back again into deep water. Hour after hour passed by.

The crews of the boats had their provisions with them, and no one at that time would think of returning to the shore for breakfast or dinner. They kept laughing and talking together, or occasionally exchanging a word with those in the boats on either side of them.

"I hope we shall have better luck than yesterday," said David Treloar. "I had made up my mind that we should have the schools if they came near us, and yet they got off again just at the time I thought we had them secured."

"You must have patience, David; trust to Him Who

helped the fishermen of Galilee when they had toiled all day and caught nothing," answered Michael. "I do not see that we should expect to be better off than they were; He Who taught the pilchards to visit our shores will send them into our nets if He thinks fit. Our business is to toil on and to trust to His kindness."

"Ah, Michael! you are always right; I do not see things as clearly as you do," said David.

"If you do not, still you know that God cares for you as much as He does for me or anyone else; and so do you trust to Him, and depend upon it all will turn out right. That's what Uncle Paul used to say, and your Uncle Reuben says."

Michael had for some time past taken pains to let it be known that he was not, as supposed to be, the son of Paul Trefusis, and had told all his friends and acquaintances the history which Paul had given him. Many of the elder people, indeed, were well acquainted with the circumstances of the case, and were able to corroborate what he said. Eban Cowan, however, had hitherto been ignorant of the fact, and had always supposed that Michael was Nelly's brother. This had originally made him anxious to gain Michael's friendship for her sake. Almost from his boyhood he had admired her, and his admiration increased with his growth, till he entertained for her as much affection as it was in his nature to feel.

No sooner was he aware of the truth than jealousy of Michael sprang up in his heart, and instead of putting it away, as he ought to have done, he nourished it till his jealousy grew into a determined and deadly hatred of one whom he chose to consider as his rival.

Michael, not aware of this, met him in the same frank way that he had always been accustomed to do, and took no notice of the angry scowl which Eban often cast at him.

Eban on this occasion had command of his father's boat.

He was reputed to be as good and bold a fisherman as anyone on the coast. Michael did not observe the fierce look Eban cast at him as they were shoving off in the morning when the two boats pulled out of the harbour together side by side.

The boats had now been waiting several hours, and when the huers were seen to raise their white boughs and point to a sandy beach to the north of the harbour (a sign that a school of pilchards was directing its course in that direction), instantly the cry of *"heva"* was raised by the numerous watchers on the shore, and the crews of the boats, bending to their oars, pulled away to get outside the school and prevent them from turning back.

Two with nets on board, starting from the same point, began quick as lightning to cast them out till they formed a vast circle.

Away the rowers pulled, straining their sinews to the utmost, till a large circle was formed two thousand feet in circumference, within which the shining fish could be seen leaping and struggling thickly together on the surface. The seine, about twelve fathoms deep, thus formed a wall beyond which the fish could not pass, the bottom being sunk by heavy leads and the upper part supported by corks. In the meantime a boat was employed in driving the fish towards the centre of the enclosure, lest before the circle was completed they might alter their course and escape.

Although the fish were thus enclosed, their enormous weight would certainly have broken through the net had an attempt been made to drag them on to the beach. The operation was not yet over. Warping or dragging them into shallow water had now to be commenced. Gradually the circle was drawn nearer and nearer the shore, till shallow water was reached. The seine was then moored, that is, secured by grappling hooks. It had next to be emptied. In bad weather this cannot be done, as the work requires smooth water. On the present occasion, however, the sea was calm, and several boats, supplied with smaller nets and baskets, entered the circle and commenced what is called *tucking*. The small nets were used to encircle as many fish as they could lift, which were quickly hauled on board in the ordinary way, while other boats ladled the pilchards out of the water with baskets. As soon as a boat was laden she returned to the shore by the only passage left open, where men stood ready to close it as soon as she had passed.

On the beach were collected numbers of women and lads, with creels on their backs ready to be filled. As soon as this was done they carried them up to the curing-house, situated on a convenient spot near the bay. Among those on the beach were Dame Lanreath and Nelly, and as Michael assisted to fill their creels he expressed his satisfaction at having contributed so materially to the success of the undertaking, for his boat had been one of the most actively employed.

As all engaged in the operation belonged to the same company, they worked with a will, each person taking his allotted duty, and thus doing their utmost to obtain success.

Some time was occupied in thus emptying the seine, for after the fish on the surface had been caught many more which were swimming lower down and making endeavours to escape, were obtained with the *tucking* nets. The whole net itself was then dragged up, and the remainder of the fish which had been caught in the meshes, or had before escaped capture, were taken out.

Such is the ordinary way of catching the pilchard on the coast of Cornwall with seines.

The inhabitants of the village congratulated themselves on their success.

Often, as has been said, tucking has to be delayed in consequence of a heavy sea for several days, and sometimes, after all, the fish have been lost.

"I mind, not long ago," observed Uncle Reuben, "when we were shooting a net to the southward, it was caught by the tide and carried away against the rocks, where, besides the fish getting free, it was so torn and mangled that it took us many a long winter's evening to put to rights. And you have heard tell, Michael, that at another time, when we had got well-nigh a thousand pounds' worth of fish within our seine, they took it into their heads to make a dash together at one point, and, capsizing it, leaped clear over the top, and the greater number of them got free. And only two seasons ago, just as we thought we had got a fine haul, and the seine was securely moored, a ground swell set in from the westward, where a heavy gale was blowing, and the net was rolled over and over till every fish had escaped, and the net was worth little or nothing. So I say we have reason to be thankful when we get a successful catch like that we have had to-day."

It was not, however, the only successful catch which Michael and his companions made that season. Still, as his boat and net were but small, his share was less than that of the rest of the company, and, after all, his share was not more than sufficient for his expenses.

A considerable number of the company were now employed in curing or bulking the late catch of pilchards. This was carried on in a circular court called a cellar. The fish which had been piled up within it were now laid out on raised slabs which ran round the court. First a layer of salt was spread, then a layer of pilchards, and so on, layers of pilchards and salt alternating, till a vast mound was raised. Here they remained for about a month or more. Below the slabs were gutters, which conveyed the brine and oil which oozed out of the mass into a large pit in the centre of the court. From three to four hundredweight of salt was used for each hogshead.

After they had remained in bulk for sufficient time the

pilchards were cleansed from the salt and closely packed in hogsheads, each of which contains about 2,400 fish, and weighs about 476 pounds. The pressure to which they are subjected forces the oil out through the open joints of the cask.

The pilchards are now familiarly called "fair maids," from *fermade*, a corruption of *fumado* (the Spanish word for *smoked*), as originally they were cured by smoking, a method, however, which has long been abandoned.

No portion of the prize is lost; the oil and blood is sold to the curriers, the skimmings of the water in which the fish are washed before packing is purchased by the soap-boilers, and the broken and refuse fish are sold for manure. The oil when clarified forms an important item in the profit.

The pilchards, however, are not always to be entrapped near the shore. At most times they keep out at sea, where the hardy fishermen make use of the drift-net.

Two sorts of boats are employed for this purpose; one is of about thirty tons burden, the other much smaller. They use a number of nets called *a set*, about twenty in all, joined together. Each net is about 170 feet long, and 40 deep. United lengthways they form a wall three-quarters of a mile long, the lower part kept down by leads, the upper floated on the surface by corks. Sometimes they are even much longer.

Within the meshes of this net the fish, as they swim rapidly forward, entangle themselves. They easily get their heads through, but cannot withdraw them, as they are held by the gills, which open in the water like the barbs of an arrow. Their bodies also being larger than the meshes, they thus remain hanging, unable to extricate themselves.

The driving-boat is made fast to one end of the wall, where she hangs on till the time for hauling the net arrives.

The fishermen prefer a thick foggy night and a loppy sea, as under those circumstances the pilchards do not perceive the net in their way. At times, however, when the water is phosphorescent, the creatures which form the luminous appearance cover the meshes so that the whole net becomes lighted up.

This is called "briming," and the pilchards, thus perceiving the trap in their way, turn aside and escape its meshes.

As briming rarely occurs during twilight, and the ocean is at that time dark enough to hide the wall of twine, the fishermen generally shoot their nets soon after sunset and just before dawn, when the fine weather makes it probable that they will be lighted up by the dreaded briming at the other hours of the night.

The operation of hauling in nearly a mile of net, with its meshes full of fish, is an arduous task, especially during a dark night, when the boat is tossed about by a heavy sea, and at no time indeed can it be an easy one. The hardy fishermen pursue this species of fishing during the greater part of the year, for small schools of pilchards arrive in the Channel as early as the month of May, and remain far into the winter, till the water becomes too cool for their constitutions, when they return eastwards to seek a warmer climate in the depths of the Atlantic, or swim off to some unknown region, where they may deposit their spawn or obtain the food on which they exist. Little, however, is known of the causes which guide their movements, and the Cornish fishermen remain satisfied by knowing the fact that the beautiful little fish which enables them to support themselves and their families are sent annually by their benignant Creator to visit their coasts, and seldom trouble themselves to make any further inquiries on the subject.

Chapter Eight.

Two more years passed away—Nelly had become a pretty young woman, modest and good as she was attractive in her personal appearance. She had admirers in plenty besides Eban Cowan, who continued, as in his younger days, to pay her all the attention in his power, and openly declared to his companions his purpose of making her his wife.

By this means he kept some at a distance who were afraid to encounter him as a rival, for they well knew his fierce and determined disposition, of which he had on several occasions given evidence. Every one knew that he and his father were leagued with the most desperate gang of smugglers on the coast, and two or three times when acting as leader of a party he had had fierce encounters with the coast-guard, and on each occasion by his judgment and courage had succeeded in carrying off the goods which had been landed to a place of safety. He frequently also had made trips in a smuggling lugger, of which his father was part owner, to the coast of France. He was looked upon as a hardy and expert seaman, as well as a good fisherman. Had he, indeed, kept to the latter calling, with the boats he owned he would have become an independent, if not a wealthy man. But ill-gotten gains go fast, and in his smuggling enterprises, though he was often successful, yet he lost in the end more than he gained.

Nelly, though flattered by the attention paid her, showed no preference for any of her admirers. She had a good-natured word or a joke for all of them, but always managed to make them hold their tongues when they appeared to be growing serious. How she might have acted without the sage Dame Lanreath to advise her, or had she not felt that she could not consent to desert her and Michael, it is impossible to say.

Michael had become a fine and active young man. As a sailor he was not inferior to Eban. He had been able to support

Nelly and her grandmother in comfort, and to save money besides. He had invested his profits in a share of Uncle Reuben's large fishing-boat, and was thus able to employ himself in the deep-sea seine fishing for the greater part of the year, as well as that of the inshore fishing which he had hitherto pursued. His only regret was that it compelled him to be absent from home more frequently and for longer periods, but then he had always the advantage of returning to spend every Sunday with Nelly.

Those Sundays were indeed very happy ones; he did not spend them in idle sloth, but he and Nelly, accompanied by her grandmother, set off early to worship together, never allowing either wind or rain to hinder them, although they had several miles to go. On their return they spent the remainder of the day in reading God's Word, or one of the few cherished books they possessed. They had received some time back two or three which were especially favoured, sent by Mrs and Miss Tremayne, with a kind message inquiring after Michael and Dame Lanreath, and hoping that the "Dove" had answered Michael's expectations and proved a good and useful sea-boat. Nelly undertook to write a reply.

"That she has, tell them," said Michael. "I often think, when I am at work on board her, of their kindness, and what I should have done had they and Mr Tremayne not given her to me."

After this, however, they received no further news of their friends, and though Nelly wrote to inquire, her letter was returned by the post-office, stating that they had left the place.

Refreshed by his Sunday rest, Michael went with renewed strength to his weekly toil.

Uncle Reuben's boat was called the "Sea-Gull." Michael was now constantly on board her, as he had from his prudence and skill been chosen as mate. When Reuben himself did not go out in her, he had the command.

75

The merry month of May had begun, the "Sea-Gull" was away with her drift-nets. Reuben hoped to be among the first to send fish to the Helston market. Dame Lanreath and Nelly, as well as several other female members of Reuben's family, or related to his crew, were ready to set off with their creels as soon as the boat returned.

Nelly had gone as far as Uncle Reuben's house to watch for the "Sea-Gull." She had not long to wait before she caught sight of the little vessel skimming over the waters before a light nor'-westerly breeze. It was the morning of the eighth of May, when the annual festival of the Flurry was to be held at Helston.

Although Nelly did not wish to take part in the sports carried on there, still she had no objection to see what was going forward, and perhaps Michael, contrary to his custom, would be willing to accompany her and her granny.

"He so seldom takes a holiday; but for this once he may be tempted to go and see the fun," she thought.

The "Sea-Gull" drew near, and Nelly knew her appearance too well to have any doubt about her, even when she was a long way off.

She now hurried home to tell Dame Lanreath, that they might be ready at the landing-place to receive their portion of the vessel's cargo.

The vessel was soon moored alongside the quay, when the creels were quickly filled with fish.

"If you will come with us to Helston, Michael, I will wait for you. Granny will go on ahead and we can soon overtake her. Though you have lived so near you have never seen a Flurry dance, and on this bright morning there will sure to be a good gathering."

"I care little for seeing fine folks dressed up in gay flowers and white dresses, and dancing and jigging, especially as neither you nor I can take a part in the fun," answered Michael. "I should like the walk well enough with you, Nelly, but a number of congers and dog-fish got foul of our nets and made some ugly holes in them, which will take us all day to mend; it is a wonder they did not do more mischief. So, as I always put business before pleasure, you see, Nelly, I must not go, however much I might wish it."

Nelly thought that David and others might mend the nets; but Michael said that he and all hands were required to do the work, and that if he did not stop and set a good example the others might be idle, and when he got back in the evening it might not be done. So Nelly, very unwillingly, was obliged to give up her scheme of inducing Michael to take a holiday, and accompanied her granny as usual.

Having left Michael's breakfast ready on the table, they set off. The dame trudged along, staff in hand; her step was as firm as it had been ten years before, though her body was slightly bent. Nelly walked by her side, as she had done year after year, but she now bore her burden with greater ease; and with her upright figure, and her cheeks blooming with health, the two together presented a perfect picture of a fish-wife and fish-girl.

Dame Lanreath had promised, after they had sold the contents of their creels, to wait some little time to see the Flurry dance and the gay people who would throng the town. Nelly looked forward to the scene with pleasure, her only regret being that Michael had been unable to accompany her.

They had gone some distance when they heard a rapid step behind them, and Eban Cowan came up to Nelly's side.

"I have been walking hard to overtake you, Nelly," he said, "for I found that you had gone on. I suppose you intend to stay and see the gay doings at Helston, and will not object to an escort back in the evening?"

"Granny proposes stopping for the Flurry dance, but we

shall come away long before it is dark, and as we know the road as well as most people, we can find it by ourselves," answered Nelly, coldly.

"You will miss half the fun, then," said Eban. "You must get your granny to stop, or, if she will not, she cannot mind your remaining with my sister and cousin, and I can see you and them home."

"I cannot let my granny walk home by herself," answered Nelly; "and so, Eban, I beg that you will not say anything more about the matter."

Eban saw that it would not do just then to press the subject, and he hoped that perhaps Nelly would lose sight of her grandmother in the crowd, and that she would then be too glad to come back under his charge. He had made up his mind to have a talk with her, and bring matters to an issue; he did not suppose that she and Michael could care much for each other, or he thought that they would have married long ago, and so believed that he had a better chance than any one else of winning Nelly Trefusis.

He walked on, trying to make himself agreeable now saying a few words to the dame, who generally gave him curt answers, and now addressing Nelly. As he had plenty to say for himself, she could not help being amused, and his conversation served to beguile the way over the somewhat dreary country they had to pass till the neighbourhood of Helston was reached.

He accompanied them in the ferry-boat which took them across to the town on the other side of the shallow estuary or lake on which it is built.

As they had now to go from house to house to sell their fish, he had to leave them, believing, however, that he should have no difficulty in finding them again when their creels were empty.

The town was at that time quiet enough, for all the shops

were closed, and most of the young men and maidens, as well as large parties of children, had gone into the surrounding woods to cut boughs and gather wild flowers.

The housewives, however, were eager to purchase their fresh-caught pilchards, to make into huge pasties, which, with clotted cream, forms the favourite Cornish dish.

They had already disposed of a considerable portion of their freight, when they saw a large party approaching along the principal thoroughfare. It consisted of a number of young people, boys and girls, their heads decked with wreaths of flowers, and holding in their hands green boughs, which they waved to and fro as they advanced, singing—

"Once more the merry month of May
Has come, and driven old winter away;
And so as now green boughs we bring,
We merrily dance and merrily sing.
No more we dread the frost and snow,
No more the winter breezes blow;
But summer suns and azure skies
Warm our hearts and please our eyes.
And so we dance and so we sing,
And here our woodland trophies bring;
Hurra, hurra, hurra, hurra!
What can with our Flurry dance compare?"

Thus the merry party went dancing and singing through the town, every one running out from their houses to greet and applaud them.

A large number of carriages and vehicles of all sorts now appeared, conveying the inhabitants of the surrounding district, who came in summer attire, decked with spring flowers, preceded by a band of music.

They all assembled before the Town Hall, when the

Flurry dance commenced. Rows of ladies and gentlemen formed opposite each other, then, moving forward, they set to each other in couples, and proceeded thus, dancing and singing, down the streets. Garden-gates stood open, and many of the doors of the larger houses. Through them the dancers entered, continuing their evolutions up and down the gravel walks and through the halls, all ranks and classes mingling together. All seemed in good humour; in spite of the exercise they were taking, none appeared fatigued or willing to stop.

The Flurry tune which was played is a peculiar one, evidently of great antiquity, and probably the custom had its origin as far back as the feast of Flora, when pagan rites were performed in the country, or, perhaps, it originally was instituted to celebrate a victory over the Saxons; or it may be a remnant of some old Celtic observance.

Few of those who took part in it cared much about its origin. The young people enjoyed the amusement of dancing and singing, and their elders their holiday and relaxation from business.

Dame Lanreath and Nelly had disposed of all their fish before the Flurry dance began; they thus had ample time to watch what was going forward, Nelly kept close to her grandmother, although she met several of her acquaintances, who stopped to have a talk, and she might easily, had she not been on the watch, have lost her in the crowd.

In the evening the grander people were to have a ball at the Town Hall; but as the dame and Nelly took no interest in watching the ladies in their gay dresses stepping from their carriages, they, having seen enough of the Flurry dance to satisfy their curiosity, set out in company with several of their friends on their walk homeward.

They were just leaving the town, when Eban Cowan overtook Nelly, who was in company with another girl a short distance behind Dame Lanreath.

"Nelly," said Eban, "I was in a great fright lest I should miss you. You are going away without seeing half the fun of the day; the people are only just getting into the spirit of the dance. I wanted you to take off that creel and have a turn with me. Among all the fine ladies there is not one can compare with you for beauty in my eyes, and many a lad there would have been jealous of me, in spite of the white dresses and bright flowers of the girls."

Nelly laughed, thinking that Eban was joking. Her companion, who believed the common report, that Eban Cowan was an admirer of Nelly Trefusis, and that she encouraged him, dropped behind and joined another party, and Eban and Nelly were left alone.

He at once changed his tone, which showed that he was deeply in earnest.

"Nelly," he said, "I have sought you for long years, and however others may admire you, they cannot care for you as I do—my love surpasses theirs a hundredfold. I can give you a comfortable home, and make you equal to any of the fine ladies we have been watching to-day. You need no longer carry that creel on your back, and slave as you have been doing, if you will become my wife. I tell you that I love you more than life itself, and ask you, will you marry me?"

Nelly would willingly have stopped Eban from talking on, but had hitherto been unable to get in a word.

"I have known you, Eban Cowan, since I way a girl, but I have never for one moment encouraged you to suppose that I would become your wife, and I now say positively that I cannot and will not. I thank you for all you have said to me, though I would rather you had left it unsaid; and I would wish to be friendly, as we have always been," she answered, firmly.

"Is that the only answer you can give me?" exclaimed

Eban.

"I can give no other," replied Nelly.

"Do you never intend to marry, then?" asked Eban.

"I am not compelled to tell you my intentions," said Nelly.

"Do you love any one else? because I shall then know how to act," exclaimed Eban.

Nelly thought for a moment. "I will tell him; it will be the kindest thing to do, as he will then understand that I can never marry him, and wisely seek another wife."

"Yes, Eban Cowan, I do love another," she said, in a low voice. "I love Michael Penguyne, and can be no other man's wife than his. You have long called him your friend; let him be your friend still, but give up all thoughts of me."

"I now know how to act," muttered Eban, gloomily. "I had no idea that you cared for him; and if you choose to become a poor fisherman's wife, you must follow your own course; only, do not suppose that I can cease to love you."

"I cannot listen to what you say," exclaimed Nelly, walking on rapidly, and feeling very indignant at Eban's last remark.

He did not attempt to follow her, and she soon overtook Dame Lanreath and the friends who were accompanying her. When she looked round, Eban had disappeared. She felt greatly relieved at having got rid of him, and she hoped that, notwithstanding what he had said, he would abandon all hopes of becoming her husband.

Eban went home by another path, muttering fiercely that he would not be balked, and that Michael should pay dearly for coming between him and the girl he loved.

People little know, when they give way to their unbridled passions, into what crimes they may be led.

Day after day Eban Cowan pondered over his rejection

by Nelly, and chose to consider himself especially ill-treated.

"She should have let me know years ago that she intended to marry that fellow. How can she think of preferring him, a poor, hard-working lad, to me?" he exclaimed; and dreadful thoughts came into his mind. He made no attempt to drive them from him.

Chapter Nine.

The autumn was drawing on. The pilchard harvest had not been as successful as the fishermen desired, and they kept their boats at sea in the hopes of obtaining a share of the schools of fish which still hovered off their coasts. The drift-nets now could only be used with any prospect of success, and Michael was as active and energetic as ever. He had, indeed, greater reason for working hard, as Nelly had promised to become his wife in the ensuing spring. He wished to make every preparation in his power that she might begin her married life with as much comfort as a fisherman's wife could hope to do.

"Only we must look after granny too, and try to save her the long trudges she has had to make; and repay her, though that would be a hard matter, for all the care she took of us when we were young," he observed to Nelly, as they were talking over their future prospects.

Nelly heartily agreed with him; but when Dame Lanreath heard of their intentions, she laughed at the notion of giving up her daily walks to market.

"More reason for Nelly to stay at home to look after the house. Wait a bit till my limbs grow stiffer than they are as yet, and till she has got a little damsel of her own to trot alongside her as she used to trot alongside me," she answered.

"But, granny, I have been thinking of getting little Mary Lanaherne, Uncle Reuben's granddaughter, to go to market with me while you stay at home; she is quite ready to agree to my plan," said Nelly.

"Ah, I see you want to become a fine lady now you are going to marry, and have an attendant of your own," said the dame, laughing. "Bide a bit till you have need of help, and let my old limbs wag on while they have life in them."

"That will be for many years to come, I hope, granny," said Michael; "and to my eyes you don't seem to have become a day older since I first remember you, and that's longer than I can remember anything else; for I mind you holding me in your arms when father came home one day and gave me a fish to play with."

"That was a good bit ago, Michael, to be sure, and I should not like to have to lift you up now, lad, strong as my arms still are," answered the old dame, looking approvingly at the fine manly young fisherman as he stood before her. Nelly, too, gave him a glance of tender affection, and all three laughed merrily. Their hearts were light, for though theirs was a life of toil they willingly undertook their daily tasks, and were thankful for the blessings bestowed on them.

"It is time for me to be off," said Michael; "Uncle Reuben stays on shore this evening, so I am to act captain. We shall be back, I hope, soon after ten, as he always wishes us to be home early on Saturday night, and as the weather looks pretty thick, and there is a nice lop of a sea on, we may expect to get a good haul."

Michael kissed Nelly's clear brow, and bestowed his usual "buss," as he called it, on granny's withered cheek; then shouldering his oilskin coat, he took his way towards the landing-place at the mouth of the harbour.

David and the rest of his crew were sitting about on the rocks with their short pipes in their mouths in readiness to go on board. Uncle Reuben had come down to see them off, and seemed half inclined to accompany them.

"If it were not for these aches in my back and sides, and that I promised my dame to stay on shore this evening, I would go with you, lads. But keep your weather eyes open. I cannot say I quite like the look of the weather. It may turn out fine, but it is very thick away to the southward."

"It will be fine enough for what we want, Uncle Reuben, and the 'Sea-Gull' does not mind a bit of a swell and a stiffish breeze, and we shall be back again almost before there is time to send a second hand to the bellows," answered Michael.

"God go with you, lads," said the old fisherman as the lads sprang on board. "If the weather gets worse, haul your nets and make the best of your way back. We will keep the light burning on the point, so that you will not miss your road into harbour at all events."

The "Sea-Gull" was shoved off, the oars got out, and, with her attendant drift-boat towing ahead, her hardy crew soon swept her out of the harbour. Her tanned sails were then hoisted, and, close-hauled, she stood away to beat up to her intended fishing-grounds some distance to the southward, off the Gull Rock.

The old fisherman stood watching her for some time, more than once saying to himself, "I wish that I had gone, the trip would not have hurt me; but Michael is a careful lad, and, even if the weather does come on bad, he will not risk staying out longer than is prudent."

Bad, indeed, there shortly appeared every probability of the weather becoming. Dark green seas came rolling in crested with foam, and breaking with increasing loudness of sound on the rocky shore; the wind whistled and howled louder and louder.

Uncle Reuben buttoned up his coat to the chin as he gazed seaward. At last his daughter came to call him in to tea.

"Mother says you will be making yourself worse, father, standing out in the cold and damp."

He obeyed the summons; still he could not help every now and then getting up and going to the door to see what the weather was like; each time he came back with a less favourable report.

As it grew dark, in spite of his dame's expostulations he again went out and proceeded to the point, where he was also joined by three or four men, who had come either to attend to the beacon which was kept burning on dark nights, or to look out for the fishing-boats which they expected would at once return in consequence of the bad weather which had now in earnest set in.

As soon as Michael had left his home, a young girl, the child of a neighbour who lived further up the harbour in the direction of the mill, came running to the cottage, saying that her mother was taken ill, and that as her father and brothers were away fishing, there was no one to stay with her while she went to call for the doctor.

Nelly at once offered to go and stay with the poor woman, and to do her best.

"No, I will go," said Dame Lanreath; "maybe I shall be able to tell what is best to be done as well as the doctor himself. Do you run on, Nancy, and I will come and look after your mother."

As the dame was not to be contradicted, Nelly continued the work in which she was engaged, and her grandmother set off with active steps towards her neighbour's cottage.

Nelly had not been long alone when she heard a hasty footstep approaching. The door opened, and Eban Cowan stood before her. A dark frown was on his brow, his eyes she thought had a wild and fierce expression she had never before seen them wear. Her heart sank within her, and she in vain tried to speak in her usually friendly tone.

"Good evening, Eban; what brings you here at this hour?" she said, on seeing him stand gazing at her without uttering a word.

"Nelly, I have come to ask you a question, and as you answer it you will make me more happy than I have been for many a long day, or you will send me away a miserable wretch, and you will never, it may be, see me again."

"I shall be sorry not to see you again, Eban, for we have been friends from our earliest days, and I hoped that we should always remain so," answered Nelly, mustering all the courage she possessed to speak calmly.

"That is what drives me to desperation," he exclaimed. "Nelly, is it true that you are going to marry Michael Penguyne?"

"I hope so, if it is God's will, as you ask me to tell you," said Nelly, firmly. "I fancied that you were his friend, as you always were mine. And, Eban, I pray that you may not feel any ill-will towards either of us, because we love each other, and are sure we shall be happy together."

"Is that the only answer you have to give me?" exclaimed Eban, hoarsely.

"I can say nothing more nor less," said Nelly, gently. "I am very sorry that my answer should make you unhappy, but you insisted on having it, and I can say nothing more."

Eban gazed at her for a moment, and appeared to be about to utter a threat, but he restrained himself, and turning hastily round rushed out of the cottage.

She was thankful that he had gone, yet a feeling of undefined fear of what he might do in his present angry mood stole over her. She was well aware of his fierce and daring character, and she had heard from her granny of desperate deeds done by men whose addresses had been rejected by girls whom they professed to love.

She earnestly wished that the dame would soon come back, that she might tell her what had occurred and consult what was best to be done.

Had Nelly known what was passing in the dark mind of Eban Cowan she would indeed have had cause for alarm.

Instead of going homewards he proceeded down towards the mouth of the harbour. On turning the point he scanned the spot where the fishing-vessels lay at anchor, and observed that the "Sea-Gull," among others, was away.

"She will be back early to-night," he muttered, "and Michael will pass this way homeward by himself, but his home he shall never reach, if I have my will. I am not going to let him come between me and the girl I have all my life intended to marry; he has no right to her: she is too good for a poor hard-working fisherman like him, and he will make her drudge all the best days of her life. If he were out of the way she would soon come round and look on me as she used to do."

Much more to the same effect he thought, working himself up to do, without compunction, the fearful act he meditated.

The pathway between the quay at the mouth of the harbour, where the fishing-vessels landed their cargoes, and Michael's house, at one place between the cliffs and the water, became so narrow that two people could with difficulty pass each other. Close to this spot, however, there existed a hollow in the rock, in which a person standing was completely concealed, especially on a dark night, when it might be passed by without discovering that any one was within.

Eban Cowan stood for some time watching the distant horizon, and as the evening drew on he observed through the gloom two or three fishing-boats running under close-reefed sails for the harbour's mouth.

"One of those is the 'Sea-Gull'; I must not be seen in the neighbourhood, or I may be suspected," he muttered, taking his way towards the lurking-place from which he intended to rush out and commit the crime he meditated.

Satan, ever ready to encourage those who yield to his instigations, persuaded him that he could do the deed without being discovered, and again and again he thought of the happiness he should enjoy with the pretty Nelly as his wife, as if the soul guilty of the blood of a fellow-creature could ever enjoy happiness!

There he stood listening amid the roar of the fast-rising gale for the step of his victim. Suddenly he thought—

"But suppose she hates me, I shall have done a deed and gained nothing. She may suspect that I did it. Why did I madly go and see her this evening? I had not intended to enter the cottage. Had the dame not gone away I should not have thought of it. Still, neither she nor any one else can swear that I am guilty. No eye will see me. The path is slippery: it will be supposed that he fell into the water." Then at that moment a voice seemed to whisper to him the words Michael had uttered long before, "God sees and hears and knows everything we do or say or think." It seemed to be that of Michael, "The darkness is no darkness to Him; the day and night to Him are both alike."

"Oh, He sees me now; He knows what I am thinking of."

The strong, daring smuggler trembled.

"I cannot do it; miserable I may be, but I should be more miserable still if I had it ever present to my mind that I had killed in cold blood another man who never wished to offend me."

He rushed from his concealment and threw the weapon he had hitherto clutched in his hand far away into the water.

He was hurrying homewards, when he heard shouts coming up from the harbour's mouth. He caught the sounds; they were cries, for hands to man a boat.

Constitutionally brave, he was ready at that moment for any desperate service. He wanted something to drive away the fearful thoughts which agitated his mind; he dreaded being left to himself; he must be actively engaged or he should go mad, if he was not mad already.

He hurried to the quay, alongside which a boat, kept ready for emergencies, was tossing up and down; she was not a life-boat, but still one well fitted to encounter heavy seas, and was used to go off to vessels which had got embayed or ran a risk of being driven on shore.

"I am ready to go off, if you want another hand," he exclaimed.

"You will do, and welcome. Our number is now made up," answered Uncle Reuben, who was seated in the stern of the boat.

Eban leaped in.

"Whereabouts is the vessel in danger?" he asked. "I could not make her out."

"She is my craft, the 'Sea-Gull,'" said Uncle Reuben. "The 'Favourite,' which has just come in, saw her driving, with her mast gone, towards the Gull Rock, and if she strikes it there is no chance for her or the poor fellows on board. Lord be merciful to them! we must do our best to try and save them, for no craft under sail will dare to stand near them, for fear of sharing their fate."

Eban knew that Michael had gone away in the "Sea-Gull." Should he risk his life to try and save that of his rival? He felt inclined to spring on shore again. The next instant Uncle Reuben gave the order to get out the oars.

Once actively engaged Eban no longer wished to quit the boat, but the wild thought rose in his mind that Michael might be lost, and then, his rival removed, that Nelly would become his.

In his selfishness he did not consider the grief she whom he professed to love would suffer; he, at all events, would not have inflicted it. He had not committed the crime he meditated, and yet might gain the object of his wishes.

Nelly had been anxiously waiting the return of Dame Lanreath; she was greatly agitated by Eban's visit—unable to overcome the fear that he might do something desperate, but what that might be she could not tell.

She frequently went to the door to see if her granny was coming.

The night drew on, the fury of the storm increased. She thought of Michael on the raging ocean engaged in hauling in his nets. The "Sea-Gull" would surely not remain out long in such weather; the fishing-vessels ought to be back by this time. She longed to run down to the harbour's mouth to ascertain if they had returned; then her granny might come in, and, finding her gone, not know what had become of her. The thought, too, that she might meet Eban in his angry mood restrained her.

"Oh, what is going to happen?" she exclaimed, feeling more anxiety and alarm than she had ever before experienced. "O my dear, dear Michael, why don't you come back to me? O merciful God, protect him!" She fell on her knees, hiding her face in her hands, and prayed for the safety of him who was on the foaming waters.

She thought she heard her granny coming. She rose from the ground and, going to the door, looked out. No one was there; she heard the roaring of the breakers on the rocky coast, and the fierce wind howling up the wild glen, making the surface of the harbour bubble and hiss and foam, and sending the spray, mingled with the cold night wind, high up, even to where she stood.

"I must go and learn why he does not come," she exclaimed. "Oh, how I wish granny would come back! she may suffer harm coming along the rough path this bleak night in the dark."

Poor Nelly felt in truth forlorn; but hers was a brave heart, which a fisherman's wife needs must have, or she could not endure the agitating suspense to which she must day after day throughout her life he exposed, when the tempest howls and the wild waves roar. She went in and put on her hood and cloak. In vain she strove to restrain her agitation. Again she went to the door. She thought she saw through the thick gloom a figure approaching.

"Is that you, dear granny?" she cried out.

"Ay, Nelly, though I have had a hard battle with the wind," answered Dame Lanreath, in her usually cheery voice. "But my journey is ended, and it was well I went to poor Polly Penduck when I did, for she was in a bad way; the doctor, however, has been with her, and she is all right now."

Nelly had run forward to lead her grandmother into the house, and she spoke the latter words on her way.

"Why, my child, what is the matter with you?" exclaimed the dame, as she saw her pale and agitated countenance.

Before Nelly could answer, footsteps were heard outside. She hurried back to the door.

"Oh! can it be Michael coming?" exclaimed Nelly. "Michael, Michael, are you there?"

"No, we be Paul and Joseph Penduck," answered two young voices. "We are on our way home to mother."

"Your mother is well and sleeping, but do not make a noise, lads, when you go in," exclaimed Dame Lanreath, who had followed Nelly to the door. "Why are you in such a hurry?"

"We needs be to get out of the storm, dame," answered one of the boys. "Father told us to make haste home; but he has gone off in the 'Rescue' with Uncle Reuben Lanaherne to look after the 'Sea-Gull,' which they say has lost her mast, and was seen driving on the Gull Rock; there is little hope of any of the poor lads escaping aboard her."

"What is that you say," shrieked poor Nelly; "the 'Sea-Gull' driving on shore?"

"I forgot, Mistress Nelly, that Michael Penguyne was aboard her," answered the thoughtless boy. "I would not have said it to frighten you so, but it may be father and the others will find them if they are not all drowned before they get there."

"O granny, I was afraid something dreadful was happening," exclaimed Nelly, gasping for breath. "I must go down to the harbour's mouth. I do not mind the wind and rain; don't stop me, granny," for Dame Lanreath had taken Nelly's arm, thinking she was about to fall, she trembled so violently. "Let me go, granny, that I may hold him in my arms, and warm him, and breathe into his mouth when he is brought on shore. Oh, I shall die if I stay at home, and he out struggling maybe for life in the cold foaming seas."

"But the lads may be mistaken, dear Nelly," urged Dame Lanreath; "it may not be the 'Sea-Gull' that has met with the damage, and if she has Michael and the rest, who are stout lads and know how to handle her, they may manage to keep her off the rocks, and get in safe notwithstanding."

Nelly, however, was not to be reasoned with. She knew the way to the harbour's mouth in the darkest night as well as by daylight; the rain and wind were nothing to her, and if Michael had got safe on shore her anxiety would the sooner be set at rest, and she should be ready to welcome him.

The dame, finding that she could not persuade Nelly to remain at home, insisted on accompanying her, for though she had tried to make her believe that Michael would return in safety, she herself could not help entertaining the fear that he had shared the fate of the many she had known in her time who had lost their lives on the treacherous ocean.

Nelly was not selfish, and though she felt that she must go forth, she was anxious that her granny should not again face the cruel storm. The dame, however, was determined to go, for she felt scarcely less anxiety than Nelly.

"Well, Nelly," she said at length, "if you won't let me go with you, I will just go by myself, and you must stay at home till I come back and tell you that Michael has got on shore all safe."

Nelly yielded. She and the dame set off.

They had a fierce battle to fight with the storm, which blew directly in their faces. They worked their way onwards, holding their cloaks tight round them.

They at last reached the rocky point where, by the light of the beacon, they saw a group of men and women and boys and girls collected, with their gaze turned seaward, waiting anxiously for the appearance of the boat which had gone out over the dark and troubled ocean in search of their missing friends.

The dame and Nelly anxiously inquired what had happened. The answer made their hearts sink: the "Sea-Gull" had last been seen driving towards the rocks in an almost helpless condition; she might drop an anchor, but there was little expectation that it would hold. The only hope was that she might be reached before she was finally dashed to pieces, and those on board her had perished.

Chapter Ten.

The "Rescue" gallantly made her way amid the dark foam-crested seas, which rolled in from the westward, each appearing heavier than its predecessor.

Uncle Reuben kept gazing out ahead in anxious search of his little vessel, now encouraging his crew with the hopes that they would soon reach the spot which she must have reached, feeling his own heart, however, sink within him as he sought in vain to find her across the wildly tossing waters. The men needed no encouragement: they knew as well as he did that every moment was precious, and yet that after all they might arrive too late. Eban pulled as hard as the rest; he would do his utmost to save the crew of the "Sea-Gull," yet he darkly hoped that their efforts might be vain.

On they pulled; often Reuben had to turn the boat's head to breast a threatening sea which, caught on the broadside, might have hurled her over. Now again he urged his crew to redoubled efforts during a temporary lull.

For some time he had been silent, keeping his eye on a dark spot ahead. It must be the "Sea-Gull." She was already fearfully near the rocks. The water there was too deep to allow her anchor to hold long, if holding it was at all. Another fierce wave came rolling towards them. Eager as Uncle Reuben was to make his way onward, he was compelled to put the boat's head towards it, and to give all his attention to avoid being buried beneath the foaming billows. The boat rose safely to its summit. A glance seaward told him that now was the time once more to make way to the south. He looked eagerly for his little vessel; the same sea had struck her. He caught but one glimpse of her hull as she was dashed helplessly against the rocks. Still some of those on board might escape. Every effort must be made to save them. Though Reuben told his crew what had happened, none hesitated to pull on.

The boat approached the rock, her crew shouted to encourage those who might be clinging to it.

The "Sea-Gull" had struck on the northernmost point, within which the sea, though surging and boiling, was comparatively quiet; and Reuben was thus enabled to get nearer to the rock than he could have ventured to do on the outside, where it broke with a fury which would quickly have overwhelmed the boat.

Two men were distinguished through the gloom clinging to the rock, at the foot of which fragments of the hapless "Sea-Gull" were tossing up and down in the foaming waves. Another sea such as that which wrecked their vessel might at any moment wash the men from their hold. A rope was hove to them, they fastened it round their waists and were dragged on board. They proved to be Reuben's two sons.

The father's heart was relieved, but he thought of his brave young captain.

"Where is Michael, where are the rest?" he exclaimed.

"Gone, gone, father, I fear!" was the answer.

"No, no! I see two more clinging to a spar!" shouted one of the men. "The sea is carrying it away, but the next will hurl it back on the rocks, and Heaven protect them, for the life will be knocked out of their bodies."

To approach the spot in the boat, however, was impossible without the certainty of her being dashed to pieces.

"Here, hand the bight of the rope to me," shouted Eban, starting up; "I am the best swimmer among you—if any one can save them I can."

As he uttered the words he sprang overboard, and with powerful strokes made his way towards the drowning men, while the rest, pulling hard, kept the boat off the rocks, to which she was perilously near.

"Here, here, take him, he is almost gone," said one of the

men in the water, as Eban approached them. "I can hold on longer."

Eban, grasping the man round the waist and shouting to those in the boat, was hauled up to her stern with his burden. Reuben, assisted by the man pulling the stroke oar, lifted the rescued man into the boat, and Eban once more dashed off to try and save the other.

"Who is it? who is it?" asked the crew, with one voice, for the darkness prevented them from distinguishing his countenance.

No one replied. Reuben hoped it might be Michael—but all his attention was required for the management of the boat, and the rescued man, exhausted, if not severely injured, was unable to reply himself.

Eban was gallantly striking out towards the man who still clung to the spar, but he had miscalculated his strength—he made less rapid way than at first. A cry reached him, "Help, mate! help!" He redoubled his efforts; but before he could reach the spot he saw a hand raised up, and as he grasped the spar he found that it was deserted. The brave fellow, whoever he was, had sacrificed his own life to save that of his drowning companion.

Eban, feeling that his own strength was going, shouted to those in the boat to haul him on board, and he was himself well-nigh exhausted when lifted over the side. One of Reuben's sons took his oar.

All further search for their missing friends proved in vain, and though thankful that some had been saved, with sad hearts they commenced their perilous return to the harbour.

Reuben's younger son, Simon Lanaherne, had gone aft and sat down by the side of the rescued man.

"He is coming to, I believe."

"Which of the poor lads is he, Simon?" asked his father.

Simon felt the man's face and dress, bending his head

down to try and scan his features.

"I cannot quite make out; but I am nearly sure it is Michael Penguyne," answered Simon.

"I am main glad if it be he, for poor Nelly's sake," said Reuben. "Pull up your starboard oars, lads, here comes a sea," he shouted, and a tremendous wave came curling up from the westward.

The attention of every one was engaged in encountering the threatened danger.

"Michael Penguyne! have I saved him?" muttered Eban Cowan, with a deep groan. "He was destined to live through all dangers, then, and Nelly is lost to me. Fool that I was to risk my life when I might have lot him drown. No one could have said that I was guilty of his death."

Human ear did not listen to the words he uttered, and a voice came to him, "You would have been guilty of his death if you could have saved him and would not."

He had recovered sufficiently to sit up, and, as he gazed at the angry sea around, his experienced eye told him that even now he and all with him might be engulfed beneath it ere they could reach the shore.

Nelly and her grandmother stood with the group of anxious watchers near the beacon-fire, straining their eyes in a vain endeavour to pierce the gloom which hung over the ocean. They could hear the sea's savage roar as it lashed the rocks at their feet and sent the spray flying over them; but they could only see the white crests of the waves as they rose and fell, and every instant it seemed to their loving hearts that these fierce waves came in with greater force than heretofore.

Could the "Rescue," stout and well-formed as she was, live amid that fierce tumult of waters? Might not those who had bravely gone forth to save their fellow-creatures, too probably perish with them?

Still, notwithstanding their fears, they listened hoping to hear the cry which those in the boat would raise as they drew near the shore, should success have attended their efforts. Again and again they asked each other, if the boat would not now be returning? Oh! how long the time seemed since they went away! A short half-hour had often sufficed to go to the Gull Rock and back. An hour or more had elapsed since the "Rescue" left the harbour, and no sign of her could be discerned.

"We must take into account the heavy seas she will have to meet; they will keep her busy for a goodish time with her bows towards them," observed an old fisherman. "Uncle Reuben knows what he is about, and if there is a man can steer the 'Rescue' on a night like this he can. A worse sea, in which a boat might live, I never saw. There is little likelihood of its getting better either, by the look of the sky."

The last remark was not encouraging; still, while a possibility remained of the return of the boat, none among the anxious group would, in spite of the rain and spray and fierce wind, leave the point.

At length a sharp-eyed youngster darted forward to the extreme end of the rock, at the risk of being washed off by the next breaker which dashed against it.

"I see her! I see her!" he shouted.

There was a rush forward. Dame Lanreath held her granddaughter back.

"You cannot bring them in sooner, Nelly," she said, "and, my child, prepare your heart for what God may have ordered. Seek for strength, Nelly, to be able to say, 'Thy will be done!'"

"I am trying," groaned Nelly; "but O granny, why do you say that?"

"It is better to be prepared for bad tidings before they come," answered the dame; "but it maybe that God has willed that Michael should be saved, and so let us be ready with a grateful heart to welcome him; but whichever way it is, remember that it is for the best."

The dame herself, notwithstanding what she said, felt her own heart depressed.

A simultaneous shout arose from the men and boys who had gone to the end of the point.

"The boat! the boat! It is her, no doubt about it," they cried out, and then most of them hurried away to the landing-place to welcome their friends and assist them on shore.

The dame and Nelly followed them. Some still remained at the point, knowing that there was yet another danger to be passed at the very entrance of the harbour, for a cross sea breaking at its mouth might hurl the boat, in spite of the efforts of the rowers, against the rocks, and those who had toiled so long, worn out with fatigue, would require assistance, for, unaided, their lives might be lost.

As the boat drew near her crew raised a shout in return to the greeting, of their friends. Perfect silence followed as the "Rescue" neared the dangerous point. In an instant it was passed, though a sea breaking over her deluged the crew.

"Are they all saved?" shouted several voices.

"Some, but not all; but our boys are here: tell my dame," shouted Reuben as the boat glided by.

Nelly heard the answer. With trembling knees she stood on the landing-place supported by Dame Lanreath, while the light of several lanterns fell on the boat and the figures of those in her as she came alongside.

Eager hands were ready to help the well-nigh exhausted crew on shore. Nelly tried to distinguish the countenances of the men—the light falling on her pale face as she stooped over.

"He is here, Nelly; Michael is safe," cried Uncle Reuben, and Simon, with two or three others, speedily assisted Michael on shore.

Nelly, regardless of those around, threw her arms round his neck, and kissed his lips and cheeks, while the dame with others helped him to move away from the quay.

"I shall soon be strong again, Nelly," he whispered. "God be praised for His mercies to us. My sorest thought was, as I felt myself in the breakers, that you and granny would be left without me to help you."

At the moment that Nelly's arms were about her betrothed, a man in the boat, refusing the aid of others, sprang on shore. As he passed, Dame Lanreath caught a glimpse of the haggard features of Eban Cowan. He rushed on without stopping to receive the greetings of any of those gathered on the quay, and was quickly lost to sight as he made his way up the glen.

"Eban seems in a strange mood," observed Simon. "He might have stopped till Michael and all of us had thanked him for his brave act; he seems as if he was sorry he had done it, or was wishing that he was with the other poor fellows who are lying out there among the rocks."

Michael was too weak to walk. Uncle Reuben invited him to come to his cottage; but he wished to return home, and there was no lack of willing arms to carry him.

"Where is David Treloar?" he asked. "If it had not been for him I should have been washed off the spar, but he held me on till I was hauled on board."

"David! poor fellow! he is among those who are gone," was the answer. "If it was he who was on the spar with you, he would not, it seems, quit it till he thought you were safe; and meantime his strength must have gone before help could reach him."

"Then he lost his life to save mine," said Michael, deeply grieved. "And how was I saved?"

"By that brave fellow, Eban Cowan, who jumped

overboard, and brought you on board," answered Uncle Reuben.

"Where is he, that I may shake him by the hand, and thank him?" inquired Michael; but Eban was not to be found.

Michael hoped the next morning to be able to go to the mill and thank Eban.

Nelly wondered at what she heard, recollecting Eban's visit to her a few hours before; but she said nothing. Indeed, by that time, with a sail, a litter had been rigged, on which his friends carried Michael to his cottage, Dame Lanreath and Nelly following them.

The rest of the population of the village hastened to their homes, several with hearts grieving for those who had been lost. They did not, however, find any lack of friends to comfort them —for all could sympathise where all knew that the like misfortune might some day happen to themselves. Uncle Reuben, too, had ample cause for grief. The little vessel on which he depended for the subsistence of his family had gone to pieces, and it would be a hard matter to obtain another. And honest David and the other lads in whom he was interested were gone; but his young boys were saved, and he felt thankful for the mercies granted him.

Michael, carefully watched over by Nelly, and doctored by the dame, soon recovered his strength. As soon as he was strong enough, he told Nelly that he must go and tell Eban how thankful he was to him for saving his life.

Nelly, on this, gave him an account of what had occurred on that eventful evening of the wreck. He was greatly astonished.

"But he is a brave fellow, Nelly; and though I cannot say what I should have been ready to do to him had I known it before, yet he saved my life, and risked his to do so, and I must not forget that. I must forget all else, and go and thank him heartily."

"Go, Michael," said Nelly, "and tell him that I bless him

from my heart, and wish him every happiness; but do not ask him to come here. It is better for his sake he should not be seeing me and fancying that I can ever care for him."

Michael promised to behave discreetly in the matter, and set off.

The heavy gale was still blowing. He wondered as he went along how the path was so much steeper and rougher than it used to be, not aware how greatly his strength had decreased.

On reaching the mill he saw old Cowan standing at the door. He inquired for Eban.

"Where is he? That's more than I can tell you, lad," he answered. "He went away the other evening and has not since come back. I do not inquire after his movements, and so I suppose it is all right."

Michael then told the old man of the service his son had rendered him.

"Glad he saved thy life, lad; he is a brave fellow, no doubt of that; but it is strange that he should not have come in to have his clothes dried and get some rest."

None of the household could give any further account of Eban.

Michael, again expressing such thanks as his heart prompted, returned home.

Several days passed and rumours came that Eban had been seen on the way to Falmouth: and his father, who had become anxious about him, setting off, discovered that he had gone on board a large ship which had put in there to seek shelter from the gale. He had left no message, and no letter was received by any of his family to say why he had gone, or what were his intentions for the future.

During the winter two or three seizures of smuggled goods were made; they belonged to the band of which Eban was supposed to have been the leader: and old Cowan, whose venture it was known they were, became gradually downcast and desponding. His fishing-boats were unsuccessful; he offered one for sale, which Uncle Reuben and Michael purchased between them; another was lost; and, his mill being burned down, he died soon afterwards broken-hearted, leaving his family in utter destitution.

In the spring Michael and Nelly married. The wedding, if not a very gay one, was the merriest which had occurred in the village for many a day, nor were any of the usual customs in that part of Cornwall omitted.

Dame Lanreath declared that she felt younger than she had been for the last ten years, or twenty for that matter, and Uncle Reuben had recovered from his rheumatism with the warm spring weather. The pilchard harvest in that year was unusually early and abundant, and Michael was able to increase the size of his house and improve its appearance, while he gave his young wife many comforts, which he declared no one so well deserved. No one disputed the point; indeed, all agreed that a finer and happier young couple was not to be found along the Cornish coast.

They were grateful to God for the happiness they enjoyed, and while they prayed that it might be prolonged, and that their lives might be spared, they did not forget that He Who had the power to give had the right to take away. But, trusting to His mercy and loving-kindness, they hoped that He would think fit to protect them during their lives on earth, while they could with confidence look forward to that glorious future where there will be no more sorrow and no more parting.

The End.

Lightning Source UK Ltd.
Milton Keynes UK
UKHW020208111019
351392UK00006B/295/P